"There's something I'd like to ask you."

Morgan smiled at her. "Ask away."

She took a deep breath. "Well, we're drifting pretty aimlessly, wouldn't you say?"

He sighed. "Nora, we've been through all that. I've already explained—"

"Yes, I know about your explanations. But they don't make sense." She gathered her courage. "I have to know, Morgan. Do you really care anything at all about me?"

"Of course I do. In my way," he added carefully.

"Then why do you refuse to make any plans beyond the next dinner date? Why do you clam up when I ask you about your past? Caring means taking risks. I think I've done that. But it's a two-way street. I can't do it alone!"

He was silent.

Rosemary Hammond lives on the West Coast, but has traveled extensively with her husband throughout the United States, Mexico and Canada. She loves to write and has been fascinated by the mechanics of fiction ever since her college days. She reads extensively, enjoying everything from Victorian novels to mysteries, spy stories and, of course, romances.

Books by Rosemary Hammond

BARRIER TO LOVE
Rosemary Hammond

Harlequin Books

TORONTO • NEW YORK • LONDON
AMSTERDAM • PARIS • SYDNEY • HAMBURG
STOCKHOLM • ATHENS • TOKYO • MILAN
MADRID • WARSAW • BUDAPEST • AUCKLAND

Original hardcover edition published in 1991
by Mills & Boon Limited

ISBN 0-373-03266-8

Harlequin Romance first edition May 1993

BARRIER TO LOVE

CHAPTER ONE

NORA flipped through the stack of glossy photographs, her frown deepening with each one. Finally, she groaned loudly, and slammed the whole pile down on top of her cluttered desk.

"No, no, no!" she cried. "These are not what I want at all!" She fixed her short, dark-haired assistant with a malevolent glare. "How many times do I have to tell that dratted agency to quit trying to foist all these pretty boys on me?"

Gloria, a calm, phlegmatic type, cocked her head to one side, and wrinkled her forehead in an attitude of serious concentration. "Well, boss," she said judiciously, "at last count I'd say about five thousand, minimum."

Nora sighed deeply, sank down into her chair, and put her head in her hands, further loosening the already untidy bun at the back of her neck. Finally, she looked up bleakly at the patiently waiting Gloria, who shrugged her shoulders, spread her hands wide, and gave her a lopsided grin.

"Gloria, what am I going to do?" Nora wailed. "This Latimer layout has to be shot in time for the November ad campaign, and so far all I have is a rack of wonderful men's clothes and no model to put them on." She groaned again, and pushed her slipping glasses back up on her nose more securely. "It's my first really big account, and I'm going to foul it up before it even gets off the ground."

Nora had worked for the prestigious McKenzie-Phillips New York advertising agency for five years, producing spot commercials for their minor clients, then graduating a little higher up the ladder to magazine layouts, until finally, in early July—just two months ago—Mr. McKenzie himself had entrusted her with the Latimer account, giving her sole authority for the major autumn campaign.

The problem was that with authority went responsibility. It was a hectic, nerve-racking business at best, juggling the disparate and often conflicting demands of photographers, writers, designers, with their temperamental outbursts and often open hostilities. She knew she was good at her job, confident she had both the competence and stamina for it, but what was she going to do without a model to hang all those marvelous Latimer clothes on?

"You know," Gloria was saying as she went slowly through the discarded photographs once again, "some of these aren't so bad." She drew one out and set it down in front of Nora. "How about this guy? Isn't he kind of sexy?"

Nora glanced at it, hoping she might have missed a hot prospect, but the hope died abruptly when she saw yet another pretty boy, with the same sullen heavy-lidded eyes, the same full pouty lips, the same slicked-back mane of hair.

She looked up and glared at Gloria. "Sexy?" she demanded. "You call that sexy? He's about as sexy as a teenage Romeo. He looks like he's probably just out of the acne stage."

"Well, I think he's pretty," Gloria protested.

"How many times do I have to say it?" Nora asked with elaborate patience. "Pretty is not what I'm looking for."

"Well, honestly, Nora, what *are* you looking for?"

Nora got up, and began to pace around the small cluttered office, running her fingers through the thick honey-colored hair that swept back from her forehead until the bun at the back threatened to fall apart altogether. Distractedly, she drew out a pin and stuck it haphazardly back into the loose coil.

She finally stopped directly before Gloria, who was a full head shorter. She crossed her arms in front of her and gazed out of the one grimy window that looked on to the blank cement wall of the building next door.

"I'll tell you what I want," she said at last. "I want a model who looks like a man, not a spoilt little boy." She waved a hand in the air. "Oh, I can't describe it. But I'll know it when I see it."

"Well, Nora, you'll have to admit, that's not much help."

"I know. I'm not blaming you." She glanced at her watch. "I'm going to run down to the corner for a sandwich. You might as well send them all home. I can't use any of them."

"Well, all right, but what are you going to do about getting a model? The photographer's due at three o'clock."

Nora shrugged into the jacket of her brown suit, smoothed down the wrinkled skirt, grabbed her handbag, and marched over to the door. "I don't know," she replied. "The first thing I'll do when

I get back is call the agency and tell them either to send me one that looks like a real man by then, or we'll go to another agency.''

As she passed through the reception room on her way to the bank of elevators, she glanced at the models the agency had sent over that morning—about ten of them, all sitting there waiting to see her. They all had the same currently fashionable sulky look she detested. Not one of them came within miles of the image she had in mind for the Latimer man.

She strode past them to the elevator, and punched the down button. Maybe she'd just have to take the most likely-looking candidate and make him over somehow to suit her ideal. The Latimer line of men's clothing was the very best ready-to-wear on the market, beautifully cut, expensive, made of the finest materials, and for *men*, not hothouse flowers or lounge lizards or gigolos.

As she stepped into the empty elevator car, she came face-to-face with her reflection in the full-length mirror on the back wall, and frowned at what she saw. A tall woman with disheveled hair, glasses slipping down her nose again, the little dash of lipstick she'd put on that morning long since worn off, and dressed in a drab, shapeless brown woolen suit, and sensible shoes.

Quickly, she turned away, faced forward, and pushed the button for the lobby.

She felt much better after she'd had lunch, even though she'd only wolfed down a greasy hamburger. She was not a breakfast eater, and having her stomach filled seemed to quieten her nerves.

Besides, she always found the crowded, busy city streets invigorating. The noise, the bustle, the highly charged electric atmosphere, all seemed to work as a source of energy to her, especially at this time of year, late summer, when there was a slight chill in the air, a brisk breeze blowing off Long Island Sound.

By the time she arrived back at the office she was ready to tackle her model problem with renewed vigor. She'd take one more look at the photographs before she called the agency, this time focusing on bone-structure and eyes rather than overall impression, looking for raw material she might be able to transform into the image she had in mind.

When she stepped off the elevator, however, the waiting room was empty. They'd all gone. No, not quite. There was one man standing at the far end by the window, his back toward her, his hands in his pant pockets, gazing down at the panoramic view of the city spread out far below.

Just then he turned around, and her heart caught in her throat. It was him! In the flesh! Just the model she had searched for so fruitlessly. The agency must have finally got the message. She started walking slowly towards him, stopping a few feet away and narrowing her eyes to give him a closer inspection.

He was tall, with a slim athletic build, and his well-cut clothes hung on the lean frame like a dream. His face was right, too, all hard lines and sharp angles, not handsome, but then her whole theory was that a man didn't have to be handsome to be attractive to women. But he did have to be intensely male, and that was exactly what this man projected. There wasn't a trace of softness about him.

He had thick dark hair, a little long, but well cut, so that it fell naturally into place and wasn't slicked back in that detestable male version of a pompadour. His eyes were perfect, too, a clear silvery gray with darker black flecks. They were gazing back at her now in a direct, slightly quizzical look.

He was perfect! Just what she was looking for. He not only looked exactly right, but he wore clothes beautifully, with just the graceful casual air of supreme confidence she'd been searching for. The only possible drawback was that he might be a shade too old. But the lines of experience at the corners of his eyes, across his forehead and down around his mouth could easily be covered by make-up.

She smiled at him, and nodded briskly. "Okay," she said. "You'll do. Come with me, and I'll fill you in on what I want."

He raised one heavy dark eyebrow, and seemed about to say something, but with a brusque beckoning gesture she turned from him, and started walking briskly down the hall toward her office.

When she reached her door, she glanced back to see that he was following her—slowly, a good twenty feet behind, not in any particular hurry. She stood there waiting for him, tapping her foot, impatience escalating with each lagging step he took. When he stopped at the water fountain and bent over to take a drink, her irritation boiled over.

"Come *on*!" she called to him. "I've got a deadline, you know. The shooting session is set up for three o'clock, and we still have to get today's clothes fitted on you."

He raised up, took out a handkerchief from the breast pocket of his dark suit jacket, wiped his mouth carefully, then stuck it in his pant pocket. When he still made no move, Nora marched back to him, and thrust her face up close to his.

By now she was beginning to have doubts about whether she wanted this man for the job after all. The way he was taking his own sweet time made her hackles rise. She was used to temperamental models by now, but this was the first time she'd encountered one who didn't jump at the chance to pose for a major ad campaign. In fact, he seemed downright reluctant.

Then she remembered all the other models she had rejected, the steady stream of lookalike clones that had passed under her critical eye. Surely she'd interviewed every male model in New York by now. She knew she'd never find another one that would even come close. She'd just have to choke down her temper.

"Listen," she said through her teeth. "Do you want this job or don't you?" Before he could reply, she went on in a more coaxing tone, "This could be your big chance, you know. It's a major campaign, with all the Latimer big bucks behind it."

He stood gazing down at her quite calmly. The gray eyes flicked over her in an appraising manner that bordered on insolence, and Nora was just about to tell him she'd changed her mind, couldn't use him after all, when he suddenly seemed to come to life.

"Sorry," he said. "I guess I was just so—um—bowled over by your wanting me for the job I couldn't quite take it in." He grinned broadly at her, revealing even white teeth, and deepening the long, narrow clefts in his flat cheeks. "Are you always so quick to make decisions?"

"Well, yes," she said, taken aback by his easy, confident tone. "As a matter of fact, I am."

He nodded. "Well, then, shall we get on with it?"

Nora gave him a dubious look. There was something about this man that didn't quite ring true. He seemed to have seized control of the whole situation and taken the initiative right out of her hands, where it belonged, and done it so easily and naturally—and so swiftly—that she had to remind herself that she was the boss, after all. She probably shouldn't have let it show how eager she was to get him.

"Right," she snapped, in a businesslike tone. "Come on, then. There's not much time."

Gloria was in the office, standing by Nora's desk and leafing dispiritedly through the new batch of "glossies" the agency had sent over while Nora was out to lunch. She glanced up when Nora came inside, and held one up.

"This is the only one who even comes close..." she began, then stopped short, shifting her gaze to the tall man standing behind Nora, her eyes widening. "Oh. It looks like you've found someone."

"Yes," Nora replied. She turned around. "What's your name, by the way?"

"Morgan."

"Gloria, meet Mr. Morgan. This is Gloria, my right hand. She'll help you fill out all the necessary employment forms later. Right now, I want to get those clothes fitted on you."

He followed her across the hall to the large studio where all the photographing was done. It was a long room with windows all across the far wall. In front of the windows was a small platform where the set was already in place, ready for that afternoon's shoot, a facsimile of a ski lodge. There was a very realistic-looking papier-mâché stone fireplace with some easy chairs set in front of it. On the painted backdrop was a window, through which was visible a long white ski slope surrounded by tall evergreens.

Nora waved a hand toward the set as they passed by. "Today's shot is for a ski outfit, so the fit won't matter too much." She went over to a door across from the set and opened it. "This will be your dressing room."

Inside was a dressing table covered with jars of makeup, a box of tissues, various creams and lotions, and a hand magnifying mirror. Above it was a large mirror set in the wall and outlined with bare light bulbs. On one side was a rack of men's clothing on hangers and encased in transparent plastic garment bags, on the other a couch.

She glanced at his empty hands, hanging loosely at his sides. "It doesn't look as though you've brought your own makeup."

"Uh—no," he said. "I'm afraid not."

"Well, we've got everything you'll need." She stepped back and eyed him carefully, her arms crossed, her chin in her hand. "You won't need much. You already have a pretty good tan, and with your bone structure you should photograph well.''

Actually, he was perfect, but she wasn't going to tell him that at this point. Nice long eyelashes and thick eyebrows. A wide, thin mouth, firm enough to look manly, but with a sensuous fuller underlip that looked very sexy.

"Okay," she said briskly, walking over to the clothes rack. "Let's get going."

He hesitated. "What do you want me to do?"

She turned back to him, her eyes wide with surprise. "Why, get your own clothes off, of course." She thought a minute. "No, first I'd better take some measurements. Take off your jacket."

She went over to the dressing table and went through the drawers until she found a tape measure. When she turned back to him, he was hanging up his suit jacket, his back to her, his arms raised.

She stood there and stared at him, mesmerized by the way the immaculate white shirt strained against the muscles of his back. What a find! He was even better built than she'd imagined. He'd be perfect for the bathing-suit scene, nice broad, bony shoulders, tapering down to a narrow waist and practically no hips at all.

He turned around to face her, and in his shirt-sleeves he looked as good from the front as from the back. She went over to him, and had just reached her arms around him, tape in hand, to measure his chest, when she suddenly became aware of an uncomfortable sensation of warmth stealing over her.

She was so close to him now that she could smell his light musky after-shave, hear his slow, steady breathing. Her fingers began to tingle where they brushed against the thin shirt, and visions of the smooth skin underneath it rose up in her mind.

Her hands stilled, and she glanced up at his face. He was gazing over her head into the distance with a bland, unconcerned expression on his face, apparently totally at ease. She could see the almost invisible bristles on his flat cheeks, the dark flecks in the steady gray eyes, the little pulse beating below his ear along the square bony jaw.

Nora had been handling models, male and female, for her entire working career at McKenzie-Phillips. To her, they'd always been only props, of no more personal significance than the objects she used for her sets. What was going on here?

Startled by the force of her strange reaction, she dropped her hands from his body as though they'd been burned, and stepped back a pace from him.

He glanced down at her, raised an eyebrow, and gave her a crooked smile. "Want me to take off my shirt now?" he asked softly.

Nora flushed angrily, brought to her senses at last by the insinuating tone, and had just opened her mouth to dress him down, when she heard a familiar male voice calling from the outer studio. She turned around to see her boss, Robert McKenzie, walking toward them.

"There you are, Morgan," he said, his hand outstretched. He smiled at Nora. "Good, I see you've met. I was going to invite you to have lunch with us today to introduce you to *the* Latimer, but I guess you'd already gone." He glanced in some bewilderment from the man still in his shirtsleeves, to Nora, still holding the tape measure. "What's going on? Nora measuring you for one of your own outfits?''

If Nora could have died on the spot and sunk through the floor at the same time, at least she could have died happy. *The* Latimer could only mean one thing. This man she had been ordering around— telling him to take his *clothes* off, for heaven's sake, was Morgan Latimer, head of Latimer Apparel, the firm's biggest client.

She glanced from one man to the other. Both of them were gazing at her steadily, her short, rotund, balding boss with a puzzled look on his round plump face, the tall Morgan Latimer with a gleam of amusement in his gray eyes, the thin sensual mouth twitching with suppressed laughter. She went hot, then cold, and prayed they'd just leave before she fainted dead away.

However, Nora hadn't fought the good fight on the battlefields of Madison Avenue these past five years for nothing. There was no point in fainting. She'd have to face it eventually. She pushed a stray strand of hair back behind her ear, then drew herself up to her full five feet seven inches, squared her shoulders, raised her chin, and forced out a wry smile.

''I'm afraid I've made a dreadful mistake,'' she said, and was encouraged to hear how steady her voice sounded to her ears. ''I do apologize, Mr. Latimer. It's just that I've had a terrible time finding just the right model for your clothes, which, by the way, I admire very much, and when I saw you sitting there in the waiting room ...''

She broke off, with an apologetic shrug. She was beginning to babble. She knew it. It was time to shut up. She wouldn't say another word. If Robert McKenzie wanted to fire her over what was an honest mistake, then let him. Besides, it was Morgan Latimer himself who had perpetuated her stupid error. Why hadn't he told her right from the beginning who he was? It was as much his fault as it was hers. More, in fact. He'd been playing with her, like a cat with a mouse, damn him, and he could just take his job and . . .

"Actually," he was saying to her now, "I don't do any of the creative work at all. It's my brother, Owen, who comes up with all the designs. I only handle the business end of things."

Like deciding on who was to handle their advertising account, she thought grimly. By now she didn't even care. She just wanted them to get out of there so she could nurse her wounds in private.

"Well," Robert said, "we'd better leave. Our luncheon reservation is for one o'clock."

When they were gone, she waited a few minutes to give them plenty of time to get away so she wouldn't run into them again, then dragged herself back to her own office. Gloria was still there, at her own desk, just rolling one of the firm's contract forms into her typewriter.

"Say," she called when she saw Nora, "I didn't get that guy's first name. Do you know what it is?"

"Morgan *is* his first name," Nora stated flatly. "His last name is Latimer."

"Hey, that's a coincidence, isn't it?" Gloria chirped. Then she noticed the grim look on Nora's face. "It's not a coincidence, is it?" she said, in a hushed voice.

Nora shook her head. "No, and I don't want to talk about it." She went over to her desk, and picked up the new stack of photographs. "Which one of these did you think had possibilities?"

Gloria reached for the stack, pulled out one of the photographs, and handed it to her. "This one."

At first glance, it was just another pretty face, and Nora rolled her eyes, groaning audibly. But time was growing short. She had to come up with something immediately or postpone the afternoon session, which was unthinkable. She'd worked too hard to organize it. The set was in place, the clothes ready, the photographer due in just a few hours.

Out of sheer desperation, she took a closer look. The bone structure wasn't bad. He obviously photographed well. Nice eyes. If she could get him to change his hairstyle and wipe that sulky smirk off his face, he just might do.

"Okay," she said at last. "Call the agency and have them send him over right away."

"Right," said Gloria, almost sobbing with relief. She picked up the telephone and started to dial. "Let's just pray he's available on such short notice."

It was well past three o'clock when they were finally ready to start shooting. Jerry, the photographer, had been standing around impatiently, smoking one cigarette after another, while Nora and Gloria put the finishing touches on their creation.

"It's a lot like turning a silk purse into a sow's ear," Nora muttered through her teeth when the gorgeous young model was finally transformed into a semblance of her concept of ideal masculinity.

Gloria stifled a giggle. "I don't think the poor boy appreciated it either, especially when you made him wash his hair."

They were standing behind Jerry and his cameras. Nora had positioned the model, whose name was Kevin, so that he was standing beside the papier-mâché fireplace with one elbow propped on the mantelpiece, a drink in his hand. The fake flames had been turned on, the hot glaring spotlights lit, and every detail looked perfect.

"Okay," Jerry called. "Ready for the first take?"

"It looks good," Nora replied. "Go ahead."

Jerry started shooting, first the set poses with the stationary camera, then the action pieces, as Kevin went through the paces Nora had rehearsed him in so carefully. The boy was a professional, she had to hand that to him, and once he'd grasped what she wanted had been quick to alter his facial expressions from smoldering pouts to hard-eyed disdain, just the look she wanted.

It wasn't perfect, not as Morgan Latimer himself would have been, but it was the clothes she wanted to sell with the ad, after all, not the man in them. And Kevin had just the right frame for the black ski pants, fine cashmere turtleneck, and heavy pullover.

By six o'clock Kevin's makeup had begun to run under the hot lights, they were all exhausted, and Nora called for a break.

"There's a couch in the dressing room," she said to him. "Why don't you go lie down for a while? Then you can have a wash and I'll help you repair your makeup." She turned to Gloria. "You might as well go on home now. I can handle the rest by myself.''

"Are you sure? I don't mind staying. You're as tired as I am.''

Nora smiled. "Yes, but there's no point in all of us dragging around tomorrow. Besides, you've got a husband waiting for you, and I don't. If you could call and order sandwiches and coffee for the three of us before you go, that'll be great.''

While Kevin went off to rest, Gloria called the corner delicatessen for the food, Jerry covered his precious cameras, and Nora tidied up the set for the next session.

When the food arrived, she and Jerry sat down on canvas chairs by the edge of the platform. The big studio was eerily quiet. Everyone else had gone home by now. It had started to rain, and the drops pattering against the windows beat a steady tattoo in the silence as they ate.

"Well, Jerry," Nora said, when she'd wolfed down half her ham sandwich. "What do you think?''

Jerry took a long swallow of coffee, leaned back in his chair, his feet propped on the platform, and smiled wearily at her. "I think you've got a winner, Nora." He shrugged. "But then I'm no expert. I only take the pictures.''

"Yes, but you know how I value your opinion. For my money you're the best photographer in the business.''

"Wow! That's high praise coming from the best young producer in New York.''

They both started to laugh at once. Nora had worked with Jerry Fielding for five years now, since she first started at McKenzie-Phillips. She always tried to get him if he was available, and in their close working association they had become good friends. She'd learned a lot from him, and had come to count on him to give her his honest professional opinion. When she was wrong, he never hesitated to tell her, but when she was right he was unstinting in his praise. That kind of sincerity was a rare phenomenon in the cutthroat world of advertising, and Nora relied heavily on it.

He was a good-looking young man, just a few years older than Nora, probably close to thirty, but he paid as little attention to his appearance as she did her own. His shaggy auburn hair was never properly cut, his short, thick beard always needed trimming, and his standard uniform consisted of ragged jeans, stained sweatshirt and run-down sneakers.

Watching him now, she noticed how glazed his normally bright hazel eyes were, the dark hollows under them. "Are you too tired to go on?" she asked.

"Not really. How about you?"

She tucked an errant strand of hair behind her ear, and gave him a rueful smile. "To tell you the truth, I'm dead beat. Let me tell you about my day."

She launched into a detailed account of the harrowing events of the day, starting with her abortive attempts to find the perfect model, the struggle to transform Kevin into the proper image, and ending with the way she'd mistaken Morgan Latimer for a model.

By the time she finished, Jerry was doubled up with laughter, choking and spluttering so hard that Nora had to jump up from her chair to pound him on the back before he strangled himself.

"You mean to say," he got out at last, still red in the face, "that you actually told him to take his clothes off, and started taking his measurements?"

She nodded grimly. "Afraid so. Can you believe it? When Robert McKenzie appeared on the scene for their lunch date, and clued me in at last on who he really was, I could have dropped dead on the spot. Or else murdered both of them. In any case, I've never been so mortified in my life."

"At least he wasn't standing there in his jockey shorts—or worse!"

Nora rolled her eyes and threw her hands up in the air. "Heaven forbid! Wouldn't that have been great?" She started clearing away the remains of the meal. "What beats me is why he went along with it for so long the way he did."

"He was probably just having some fun with you. He has that reputation."

She turned around to face him. "Oh, really? What kind of reputation is that?"

Jerry shrugged. "Oh, you know. Man about town, carefree bachelor." He grinned. "Seducer of women." He got up, stretched, and looked down at the tray in her hands. "Say, aren't you going to finish your sandwich? We still have another three or four hours of shooting before we're through. Or are you ready to quit? You look as beat as I feel."

"No. Oh, please, no," she said hurriedly. "After today's fiasco, I've got to come through with a really super product—and bang on time—or I'll be taken off the account for sure." She wrapped the other half of her sandwich, and held it up. "I'll finish this while you're shooting the next set."

It was ten o'clock when Nora finally dragged herself up the two flights of stairs to her small apartment in the East Village. Jerry had given her a ride home, and on the way they'd made arrangements for shooting the next segment on Wednesday of the following week, the first date he was available, and her mind was already full of plans for the next set.

As she was unlocking her door, the telephone started to ring inside. Wondering who could be calling her at this hour, and hoping fervently that Jerry hadn't had an accident on his way home, she hurried inside, and snatched up the telephone in the tiny foyer.

"Hello." She tucked the receiver in her shoulder and started fastening the several locks on her door.

"Hello," came a man's voice. "May I speak to Nora Graham?"

"This is she. Who's calling?"

"This is Morgan Latimer."

Nora almost dropped the telephone. Why on earth was Morgan Latimer calling her at this hour of the night? Then her blood ran cold. He was going to fire her for her stupid behavior today. No. He'd surely have some flunky do that. Besides, it had been an honest mistake.

"I've been trying to get hold of you all evening," the low, smooth voice went on.

"I—I've been working," she stammered. On *your* account, she added silently. Where did you think I'd be?

"Ah, yes," he said. "The ad campaign. Did you find your model?"

Nora's mind raced. He didn't sound angry. In fact, there was a definite undercurrent of amusement in his voice. But then he could afford to be amused. He held all the winning cards. Maybe it would be best to make an abject apology now, before he lowered the boom.

She sank down on the chair beside the telephone table and took a deep breath. "Listen, Mr. Latimer, I'm really sorry about what happened today. You see, I have this tendency to jump to conclusions and barge into things when I'm in a rush. I hope you know that if I'd had any idea who you were, I never would have..." She broke off. She was babbling again. "Well," she ended up limply, "all I can say is that I'm very sorry if I offended you."

He laughed, a deep chuckle. "Offended me? Why should I be offended? I was very flattered, as a matter of fact." He laughed again. "It's not every day I get asked to take my clothes off by a lovely young woman."

Nora eyes widened in astonishment. Me? Lovely? She could hardly believe her ears. All her life she'd been called smart, clever, imaginative, efficient— sloppy! But never lovely.

But what did it matter? It was probably just the way men talked in his circles. The important thing was that he wasn't furious, he wasn't going to get her taken off the account, and she heaved a deep inward sigh of relief.

"Oh," she said. "That's good." But then why was he calling her? Something had to be wrong, very wrong, for an important man like Morgan Latimer to take the trouble to call her personally.

As though he could read her thoughts, he went on to explain. "The reason I called was to ask you to have dinner with me one night this week. Are you free on Saturday?"

CHAPTER TWO

NORA stared at the telephone in her hand as though it were on fire or had suddenly come alive and was about to attack her. It was the last thing she would have expected, and she hadn't a clue what to say, even what to think.

"Nora?" His voice sounded as though it were coming from a great distance. Actually, it was. In the shock, she'd yanked it away from her ear, and let it drop in her lap. "Are you still there?"

"Yes," she said faintly. "I'm still here."

"Well? Will you have dinner with me on Saturday?"

She still couldn't speak. What was she going to do? If she turned him down she might blow the account, lose her big opportunity before she had the chance to prove herself. But of one thing she was absolutely certain. It was out of the question to accept his invitation. He was so far out of her league he might as well live on the moon.

"I—I'm sorry," she managed to stammer out at last. "I'm afraid I can't make it this weekend. My father has been ill, and I've already made plans to go home to visit him."

"And where is home?" came the smooth voice.

"Oh, just a little town up in Vermont."

He hesitated for a moment. "I wonder if I could talk you into changing your plans. Couldn't you go home another time?"

Nora was tempted. She even debated for a few seconds, but she had promised her parents. "I'm afraid not," she said at last. "My parents are expecting me. I'm really sorry, Mr. Latimer."

"Morgan, please."

"Yes. Morgan."

"Well, I'm sorry too, Nora. Perhaps some other time."

"Yes. Some other time."

They hung up then, and Nora sat there in the dark for a good five minutes pondering over what had just happened. Maybe she was dreaming. She was exhausted, and had worked herself into a lather over this whole model business. She even pinched herself to make sure. No, it hadn't been a dream.

What puzzled her was what in the world had prompted him to ask her out in the first place, especially after she'd made such a fool of herself today. Then a horrible thought crossed her mind. Had he thought it was a come-on?

On an impulse, she picked up the telephone and dialed Jerry's number. On the seventh ring, when she was just about to hang up, his sleepy voice came on the line.

"Jerry Fielding here. Who the hell is calling at this hour?"

"Jerry, it's me, Nora. The craziest thing just happened."

"It had better be pretty crazy, my girl," came the terse reply. "I'd just tucked myself in bed and was heading off to dreamland."

"Morgan Latimer just called me."

"Oh? Was he upset?"

"No. In fact, just the opposite." She hesitated. "Jerry, he asked me to have dinner with him Saturday night."

There was dead silence on the line for several seconds. "I see," Jerry said at last, a new note of caution in his voice. "And what did you say?"

"Well, I said no, of course. I told him I'd already made plans to go home this weekend."

"And how did he take it?"

"Beautifully. Just said he was sorry and maybe we could make it another time." She frowned. "Jerry, you don't sound in the least surprised."

"Should I?" came the guarded reply.

"Well, I should think so!" she stated indignantly. "Why in the world would he do a thing like that?"

"Well, why not? Listen, my dear girl, beneath that frowsy exterior and those shapeless clothes is a very attractive girl. I might even say a beautiful seductive girl, if she'd only give herself half a chance."

Once again, Nora was stunned, hardly able to believe what she was hearing. She laughed nervously. "Jerry, we must have a bad connection. This is me, Nora."

"I know who it is," he said, dead serious now. "Go take a good look at yourself in your mirror. Perhaps this was just the jolt you needed to come into the real world. Now, I'm going back to bed, and I advise you to do the same. We'll talk about it tomorrow. Have lunch with me."

"Oh, I can't. Tomorrow's Friday, and I'm leaving for Vermont on the noon train."

"Okay. When you come back, then."

After she had hung up she walked slowly through the empty apartment, switching on lights as she went. In her bedroom, she went to the mirror over the dresser and stared at her reflection, Jerry's words echoing in her ears. She had to laugh out loud at what she saw. He was certainly right about the frowsy exterior, but beautiful underneath? Seductive? Never in a million years.

She raised her hands to remove the pins from her hair, so that it fell loosely around her face. Then she took off her glasses and cocked her head to one side, squinting and peering into the mirror for a closer inspection. Taken one by one, her features weren't bad, but put all together they only added up to a rather pleasant-looking young woman who appeared at the moment to be on her last legs.

So much for beauty! She turned away and started stripping off her clothes, letting them fall on the floor, went around in her nightgown switching off all the lights, then fell into bed.

The next morning Nora awoke with a throbbing head and aching muscles. She opened one sleepy eye and glanced at the bedside clock. Nine-thirty! She must have forgotten to turn on her alarm last night!

She groaned, rolled over onto her stomach, and buried her head in the pillow. Maybe she was catching something. Wouldn't that be great? No, she was just worn out from yesterday's panic. Did she really need to go into the office today? She was going home today anyway, and the visions of her mother's warm, cozy kitchen, the smell of fresh baking, her father's affectionate teasing were too tempting to resist.

She sat up in bed, thinking it over. The next photography session wasn't set up until next Wednesday. It was to be a scene with a business suit, by far the easiest set to prepare, with no unusual props. They could even use Robert McKenzie's large, bright corner office for it. Gloria could handle anything that came up now that they had successfully transformed Kevin.

The more the idea took hold, the better she began to feel. Before she could change her mind, she jumped out of bed, padded barefoot out to the telephone in the hall, her aches and pains forgotten, and dialed her office number.

"Nora Graham's office," came Gloria's pleasant voice.

"Hi, Gloria, it's me. Listen, unless Kevin has dropped dead during the night, or Jerry forgot to put film in his camera yesterday, I don't think I'll come in today at all, maybe try to make the early train to Vermont."

"Good," came the prompt reply. "There's not that much to do around here today. In fact, I'm the only one here. Everyone else is out taking advantage of what's probably the last of the summer weather."

"Thanks, Gloria. You have my parents' number. If anything really hairy crops up, you can call me. Otherwise, I'll see you bright and early on Monday."

It wasn't until she'd showered and dressed, and was packing the one small suitcase she planned to take, that she remembered the telephone call last night from Morgan Latimer. Her hands stilled, and she stared blankly down at the blouse she was folding. Surely it had been a dream. It couldn't possibly have happened.

She *did*, however, remember calling Jerry and telling him about it. Surely she wouldn't have done that if she'd dreamed it. She *had* called Jerry. She distinctly recalled the shooting date they'd set up for the following Wednesday. If it was true that Morgan Latimer had actually asked her out to dinner, it was a mystery she didn't have time to fathom at the moment if she wanted to make that early train.

She did arrive at Grand Central Station in time, but just by the skin of her teeth, running through the cavernous depot to her platform, after a mad taxi ride through the traffic-clogged streets.

She sank into the grimy plush seat by the window, still out of breath, her heart pounding, just as the train started chugging slowly on its circular route out of the city. Soon it was heading north, picking up speed. The car was crowded with the usual weekenders, intent on escaping the city for a few days. It was too early for skiing, even in the highest slopes of Maine and Vermont, but autumn came early to New England, and further north the leaves had already begun to turn.

Nora's immediate destination was Albany, the state capital. From there she would transfer to the bus that would take her directly into Wimslow, the small Vermont town just across the New York state line where she'd grown up.

They were traveling through the beautiful Hudson River Valley now, past Peekskill, Poughkeepsie, and West Point, the broad river surrounded by the steeply-sloping hills on either side. Even now the foliage on the hills was turning from green to shades of gold and rust on the tall maples, oaks, and birches, and as Nora gazed out through the sooty window at the familiar scenery a sudden glow of anticipation warmed her.

It had been several months since she'd been home. Funny how she still thought of the little town, her parents' house, as 'home,' even after five years away from it. More, counting her college days at Bennington. Living now in the exciting and constantly changing world of Manhattan, that home represented an anchor, a point of stability in her life, that she badly needed. Maybe because she'd been an only child, and so close to both her parents.

After Hyde Park, there was only another half hour to go. She leaned her head back and closed her eyes, and immediately the image of Morgan Latimer popped into her mind. And for the first time, she asked herself—if it really had happened, if he had indeed called her, did she want to go out with him? He said he'd try again.

A little tingle of excited anticipation began to crawl along her skin at the memory of those steely-gray eyes, the firm set of the jaw, the air of confidence, the calm assumption of superiority and invulnerability. And once again she had to wonder what in the world he wanted with her. Would he call her again? In a way she rather hoped he wouldn't. Surely it would be playing with fire if she were to get involved with a man like that.

On the other hand, what could he do to her, after all, except get her fired? And apparently he didn't mean to do that. She mulled over what Jerry had said about his reputation. Man about town, he'd called him. Carefree bachelor. Seducer of women. Well, so what? There wasn't a man on earth who could talk her into doing something she didn't want to do. She'd made her way in a man's world on her own merits, bypassed romance for the sake of her career. She could handle anything Morgan Latimer cared to dish out. Couldn't she?

She wished now, a little wistfully, that she'd had more experience with romance. She'd dated a lot in college, but except for one short-lived adolescent affair with a boy she'd thought she was going to marry her relations with men had never really gone beyond the stage of a few halfhearted kisses. She'd always had more interesting things on her mind, and men soon tired of a girl who would rather study or attend a seminar than go to a drunken fraternity party, or stay up all night solving the world's problems.

Then, when she'd started working at McKenzie-Phillips, she'd been plunged immediately into such a whirl of activity, with so many demands on her time, and up against such stiff competition, that there was no room for romance. There had been plenty of men available, and her friends had set her up with one blind date after another, but her heart had never been in it. Men seemed to sense that, and eventually stopped calling her.

Now she had to wonder if she'd been missing something. Here she was, twenty-seven years old, successful in her career, but with virtually no personal life at all. Self-pity began to well up in her, hovering around the edges of her consciousness.

Just then the train began to slow, and she heard the conductor calling out, "Albany. Next stop, Albany." Her eyes flew open, and she started to gather her things together. As she reached up to the overhead rack to retrieve her overnight case, she had to smile at the path her thoughts had led her into. One telephone call from a devastating man, and she was beginning to regret her whole life.

An hour later, Nora was sitting at the kitchen table, watching her mother prepare lunch while her father was bathing.

"How is Dad, really?" she asked.

Her mother turned from the soup she was ladling out. "Well, I don't mind telling you he had me worried there for a while." She laughed. "Doctors make the world's worst patients, you know, and he never did think much of Jim Preston's medical abilities."

"But it was definitely a heart attack?"

Her mother nodded. "Only a mild one. A warning, Jim called it. He plans to go back to work next week."

"Should he?"

"Jim says it's best for him to live as normal a life as possible, just so long as he doesn't overdo things."

Nora snorted. "Fat chance of that!"

Just then her father came inside the room, fresh from his bath, wearing his old navy blue dressing-gown, clean pajamas, and shabby leather slippers.

When he saw Nora sitting at the table, his eyes lit up, and he leaned down to kiss her.

"Well, we didn't expect to see you until this afternoon." He sat down across from her.

"How are you feeling, Dad?" she asked, with some concern. "Mother tells me you're planning to go back to the office next week. Do you think that's wise?"

He held up a warning hand. "Now don't you start. That's all I've heard from Jim Preston and your mother for the past week. I'm fine." He grinned broadly. "I'm not quite ready to go just yet."

The telephone in the living room rang at that moment. "Oh, drat," her mother said. "That'll be May Cowan about the church bazaar. I may be a while, so you two go ahead and eat without me."

With a sigh, she set down the bowls of steaming soup in front of them, and dashed out of the room.

"Now," her father said when she was gone, "how have you been?"

"Great," she replied. "Couldn't be better."

"Job coming along all right?"

While they ate she told him about the Latimer account she'd been given, what a lucky break it was for her so early in her career. As always, her father seemed genuinely interested, asking just the right questions to draw her out. She ended up at last with the story about mistaking Morgan Latimer for a model.

Her father found this so hilarious that she began to feel a little let down. "Go ahead and laugh," she said sternly. "But at the time it wasn't in the least funny. I could have been fired, or at least taken off the account, for a howler like that.''

''Well, you weren't, I take it,'' he said, still grinning.

She had to smile back at him. ''No. As a matter of fact, the great man himself called me that very night and asked me out to dinner. I was so shocked that I'm still wondering if it was a hallucination.''

Her father sobered instantly. ''Why should you be shocked?''

She shrugged. ''Well, after all, Dad, Morgan Latimer is one of the most important men in New York. Why would he want to bother with someone like me?'' She laughed, and ran a hand over her hair, already coming loose from its pins. ''I'm hardly the kind of beauty he usually squires around, from all reports.''

He only shook his head back and forth, slowly, for several seconds, eyeing her narrowly. ''You always did put yourself down in that department, my girl. You're not only quite a nice person, but a beautiful young woman besides. And for my money, you're good enough for any man. Too good for most of 'em.''

She had to smile. ''And you're not in the least prejudiced, are you?''

His mild blue eyes flew open. ''Who, me? Prejudiced about my only daughter? If he calls again, are you going to go out with him?''

She sighed. ''That's the very issue I've been debating ever since. To tell you the truth, I really don't know. I'll have to admit I'm tempted. He's quite a catch.''

"Well, just be careful. There are a lot of predators out there, and you haven't had much experience. At least," he amended, with a grin, "that I know about." He held up a warning hand. "And if I'm wrong, please don't tell me about it. Leave me my illusions."

Later, when she was upstairs in the bathroom washing off the grime from her trip, Nora glanced at her reflection in the mirror. Were there possibilities there she should cultivate? Her father thought she was beautiful. But that was what all loving fathers thought. Still, Jerry had said much the same thing last night. Maybe it was time she started paying attention to something besides her career.

It was at that moment, she realized later, that she made her decision. If Morgan Latimer called her again, she'd go out with him.

Two weeks later, however, he still hadn't called her. She hadn't even seen him, and by now the whole episode had begun to fade from her mind, with only a trace of lingering regret that she hadn't snatched at the opportunity when it was offered to her.

She tried to tell herself she was better off, that a man like Morgan Latimer was too rich for her blood, but an insidious little voice that wouldn't quite keep still kept telling her that, even so, it would have been an experience that possibly only came along once in a lifetime.

Even though she didn't see him in person, it seemed that everywhere she turned she heard about him. Two weeks ago she'd hardly known of his existence, except as a name, a presence behind all that lovely Latimer ad money. Now, as though she'd sprouted an invisible antenna that picked up only on his frequency, she would see his picture in the newspaper, or see his name mentioned in the gossip columns, or hear her co-workers discussing him.

The general consensus pretty well confirmed her own first impression. Just as Jerry had said, he was a well-known, highly visible man about town, always to be seen out with a glamorous model, or actress, or society deb.

The day inevitably came, however, when she did run into him. She had just come back from lunch. It was pouring with rain outside, and as usual she'd forgotten her umbrella. She had worn a raincoat, so at least her clothes were dry, but her hair was sopping wet, and the long strands that had come loose from the bun were clinging damply to her face and neck.

When the elevator doors opened, there he was, standing there waiting for it, dressed immaculately in a dark business suit and a beautifully tailored gray gabardine trenchcoat. Of all the times to run into him! For one panicky moment she debated pushing the button to close the car and go wherever it wanted to take her, up or down, it made no difference, just so that he couldn't see her, but it was far too late for that.

She lifted her chin, forced out a smile, and stepped out of the elevator. She had just opened her mouth to say hello, when he nodded distantly at her, and strode past her into the waiting car. By the time she'd recovered her senses and turned around the doors were closing, and he had disappeared from view.

"Well," she muttered under her breath. "So much for the impact I made on *him*!"

She trudged dispiritedly down the hall to her office, dripping as she went. Was he snubbing her? No, why should he do that? She wasn't that important to him. Had he not recognized her then, in her present bedraggled state? In a way she fervently hoped so, but in another it wasn't very flattering to be forgotten so quickly.

In any case, whatever small spark she'd lit in that broad masculine breast had obviously fizzled out, and her one consolation was that now she could put the whole thing out of her mind.

In late October the advance copies of the publications containing the Latimer ad were delivered. When the messenger appeared, Nora was alone in her office.

"Nora Graham?" he asked, cocking an eye at her.

"Yes."

"Package for you."

There was a choking sensation in her throat as she watched him set the bulky package, wrapped in brown paper and tied with a string, on top of her desk. Then, brisk and businesslike, in a hurry, he thrust a clipboard at her, and pointed at a line on the top page.

"Sign there, line thirteen."

Line thirteen! She shuddered, hoping it wasn't an omen, then scrawled her name and thanked the boy, who was already on his way out of the door, whistling as he went.

She stood there for a long time, transfixed, staring at the package as though it were a bomb that might go off at any moment. Then she heard voices, and looked up to see Gloria bouncing into the room, with Jerry close behind her.

"Well," Gloria said. "Haven't you opened it yet?"

Nora frowned. "My, news travels fast around here."

It was her baby, and she'd wanted to get a look at it first on her own. But when she saw the looks of eager anticipation on both their faces, she knew she was being selfish. They'd worked hard on it, too.

"Why don't you do the honors, Gloria? There are scissors in the top drawer of my desk."

"Oh, no. You do it. It's your project."

"It's *our* project."

Jerry snorted loudly, and gave them both a disgusted look. "Well, will somebody please open the damn thing? I've got a model in the studio, shivering in a bikini, waiting for me."

Finally, Nora crossed over to the desk, got out the scissors, cut the string and unwrapped the brown paper to reveal a stack of glossy magazines. With shaking fingers she quickly flipped the top one open to the ad in the front and stared down at it. She could hear Jerry and Gloria, close behind her, breathing heavily.

It was a five-page spread. First the ski outfit, then the business suit, a sailing scene, casual wear for the country, and finally a white dinner jacket. Nora turned the pages slowly. Kevin looked wonderful. There wasn't a trace of the old sulky expression on his bony face, and Jerry had outdone himself with the photography, the lighting angle perfectly set so as to direct the eye to the clothes, not the man.

"Well, Nora," Jerry said at last, in a hushed voice. "I think you have a winner."

She turned her head swiftly to face him. "Thanks mainly to you, Jerry. You did a marvelous job."

He shook his head. "No, it's all your creation." He grinned. "But, even if I do say so myself, it is some of my best work." Then, to her amazement, he leaned closer and gave her a quick peck on the cheek.

"Listen to us!" she cried. "We sound as though we've just created a great work of art. It's only an ad, after all."

"Well, yes," Jerry agreed. "But it's a damn good ad, one of the best I've seen, and that's our job, after all."

Still flushed with excitement, she turned back to the magazine, and flipped slowly through the pages again, this time with a more critical eye. It was good, but she could still see ways to improve it. Next time she'd do an even better job.

That afternoon Robert McKenzie poked his head into her office, his round face wreathed in smiles.

"I just wanted to stop by to congratulate you on the Latimer spread," he said. "You did a fine job, Nora."

Nora flushed with pleasure. "Thank you, Mr. McKenzie. But I had a lot of help. Jerry's a real artist with the camera, and I couldn't have managed without Gloria."

"Well, that's as may be, but it was your inspiration after all that put it all together. Anyway, I want you to know that the firm is very pleased with your work, and there'll be an extra bonus for you at Christmas this year."

He gave her an indulgent nod, and had just started out of the door, when he turned around. "By the way, Latimer's is quite pleased with the ad, too. In fact, so much so that they're throwing a little party to celebrate this Saturday night. Eight o'clock in their offices. It'll probably be a dressy affair, so wear something smashing."

With that, he was gone. Nora stared after him. A party? She wasn't so sure about that. She hardly ever went to parties, and certainly didn't have anything to wear that would be suitable for a gathering that would probably consist mainly of people in the fashion industry. But it was virtually a command performance. Robert McKenzie had simply taken it for granted that she'd attend. There was no way out of it.

Maybe she could get Jerry to take her. That was if she could ever get him out of those jeans and into a dinner jacket. First things first. What was she going to do about her own appearance? Today was Thursday. That gave her only two days to prepare. She'd have to take tomorrow off, the whole day. It would take her at least that long even to make a decent start.

For a complete make-over, that would mean making appointments. Hairdresser, wardrobe consultant. She might as well go for the best. She took her telephone directory, looked up the numbers, and started to dial.

* * *

On Saturday night, as Nora surveyed herself in the mirror in her bedroom, her heart sank. The person she'd been used to seeing there had disappeared. In its place was a complete stranger, a glossy version of the old Nora who could have stepped out of the pages of a magazine ad herself. She simply couldn't go through with it. She felt like an impostor, as though she were in disguise.

Her honey-colored hair was twisted into an elaborate chignon at the top of her head, sprayed and lacquered into shiny perfection, and adding at least two inches to her height. She'd had a manicure and a professional makeup job late that afternoon at one of Manhattan's most exclusive salons, and it felt just like a mask that had been glued to her face.

But the last straw was the dress. What a dress! How had she ever let that saleswoman talk her into it? Wardrobe consultant, indeed! Not only had it been outrageously expensive, costing more than she'd spent on her entire wardrobe for the past two years, but it fit her so perfectly, almost like a second skin, that she scarcely dared breathe in it, much less move around.

Still, the color was marvelous, a luscious shade of bottle green that almost exactly matched her eyes. The trouble was that it seemed so constricting after the loose shapeless clothes she wore ordinarily. And it was cut far too low. When she'd said that to the consultant, the latter had only shaken her head vigorously. "You've got the body for it," she'd said in a firm tone. "The dress was made for you."

She raised her arms and held them out, twisting her shoulders this way and that. Well, at least it didn't fall off. Still, it was far too provocative. It made her look like a call girl on the prowl. And the high-heeled gold sandals were absolutely wicked.

She sat down on the bed, and groaned aloud. What was she going to do? She couldn't go to a party dressed like this, but there was absolutely nothing in her wardrobe that even approximated a party dress. There was an old pink number she'd worn to a friend's wedding four years ago, but it probably wouldn't even fit her now, besides being hopelessly girlish in style. She'd just have to fake an illness.

Just then the doorbell rang, and she almost jumped out of the expensive dress. Jerry! She'd forgotten Jerry! After the terrible time she'd had talking him into taking her to the party, getting dressed up, she couldn't possibly back out now. She got up, squared her shoulders, and took one more look at herself in the mirror. She'd just have to bite the bullet and go through with it.

She ran down the hall to the front door, almost tripping in the new high heels, took a deep breath, and flung it open.

"It's about time," Jerry began. He stopped short and stared for several long seconds, then let out a low whistle. "What happened to you?" he asked, in an awed tone.

"Is it awful?" she asked.

Jerry stepped inside, and closed the door after him. "Awful?" He eyed her carefully. "That isn't quite the word I'd use. You look absolutely gorgeous." He grinned. "But didn't I always say a real beauty lurked beneath those shapeless suits of yours?''

"Hah!" she exclaimed, feeling better. "You're one to talk." Her eyes swept over him. "You look pretty spiffy yourself."

The dinner jacket, obviously rented, didn't quite fit him, his tie was askew, and his reddish-brown hair not quite in place. But he had made an effort, even trimmed his beard, and she was grateful. Having Jerry to lean on put the whole thing into better perspective. It was only one night, after all.

"Well," she said, gathering up her wrap. "Shall we go?"

CHAPTER THREE

NORA saw him the moment they stepped inside the enormous conference room at the Latimer offices. Even though it was already packed with people, Morgan Latimer was so much taller than most of the others that she couldn't miss the dark head.

He was standing at the far end of the room, where a bar had been set up, drink in hand, his head slightly bent toward a tall dark-haired woman who was speaking to him. From her graceful posture and the polished perfection of her appearance, she could be one of his actresses or models. In his formal black suit and gleaming white shirt, he looked more devastating than ever.

He was deeply tanned, as though he'd recently spent some time in the sun, something she'd been too flustered to notice when she'd seen him at the elevators the other day, and she had visions of a lush Caribbean island, with nothing to do all day but lie in the sun and have a good time. Of course, he wouldn't have been alone, and she wondered if the beautiful brunette had been his companion.

Suddenly, she felt Jerry grip her elbow tightly and bend his head to hers. "My, how I hate this kind of shindig," he groaned in her ear. "Come on. I need a drink."

There were several waiters wandering through the crowd, carrying trays of cocktail glasses held high over their heads. Jerry elbowed his way toward the nearest one, with Nora trailing close behind him, a little dazed by the whole thing. The din was terrific. It seemed everyone there was talking at the top of his voice, there was music playing in the background, the clink of glassware, punctuated by periodic feminine shrieks, or masculine guffaws of loud laughter.

When they finally reached the waiter, Jerry grabbed a double Martini off the tray, and turned to Nora. "What'll you have?"

"Is there any wine?"

"Sure." He grinned. "From the bottles I noticed sitting on the bar, I'd say vintage champagne. Nothing but the best for Latimer's."

They took their drinks over to a relatively empty corner of the room and stood there for a few minutes, pressed against the wall, watching the bustling activity. Nora sipped on her wine while Jerry downed half his Martini in a quick gulp. When another waiter passed close by, Jerry finished what was left in his glass, set it down on the tray and grabbed another, all in one sweeping motion.

Nora gave him a look. "You keep on like that and I'm going to have to wheel you home."

"Don't nag," he said, taking a healthy swallow.

"Okay." She shrugged. "I can always take a cab home." She gazed out over the crowd. "Who *are* all these people? I don't see one familiar face."

At that very moment, as though on cue, her eyes lit on the tall male's dark head. He was still right across at the other end of the room. At that moment, he looked up, and, although their gaze met for a split second, before Nora quickly glanced away, there was no sign of recognition in the silvery-gray eyes.

"You know what your trouble is," Jerry was saying. "You haven't had enough to drink yet. Come on, finish that up and have another."

Nora eyed him dubiously. "Are you trying to get me drunk, Jerry?"

"Uh-uh," he said with a firm shake of his red head. "I never mix business with pleasure."

Nora had to laugh. Jerry's affairs with his models were legendary in the fashion business. "Good idea," she murmured.

Just then a tall blond Adonis came walking toward them, making his way purposefully through the crowd, his bright blue eyes firmly fixed on Nora.

"Hello, Jerry," he said, sticking out his hand. "Long time no see."

Jerry shook his hand. "Hello, Warren," he said. He turned to Nora. "Do you know Warren Carruthers?" Nora shook her head. "Warren, meet Nora Graham. She's with McKenzie-Phillips. Warren's mother is Renée Carruthers Cosmetics."

While Nora chatted with the handsome blond man, two more friends of Jerry's, also photographers, appeared out of nowhere, ogling Nora, both of them obviously intent on an introduction, and it was only a matter of seconds before a small cluster of men had formed around her.

Nora stood there sipping on champagne and basking in the glow of all this masculine attention, while Jerry moved off to one side, his eyes darting around the huge room, which seemed to be full of beautiful people, male and female. Finally, after he'd gulped down three double Martinis in a row, he murmured his excuses, and went off in hot pursuit of a lissom redhead.

Nora watched him go in some dismay. While it was a heady experience to be surrounded by admiring men with Jerry safely at her side, once he was gone she began to feel a little nervous, even rather bored with the whole thing. The men were all so alike, sizing her up quite openly, with the same suggestive banter, the same unmistakable glint of the chase in their eyes.

"Can I get you another drink?" Warren Carruthers asked her, leaning a little closer. "Or something to eat?" He gestured toward the long, white-linen-covered buffet table set against the wall.

"No, no, thanks, Warren."

Then she smiled sweetly, murmured something vague about the powder room, and simply walked off. Her feet hurt in the new sandals, and, even in the bare dress, the room had grown so warm that she was beginning to feel rather faint. They'd only been there less than an hour, and she'd already drunk three glasses of champagne, which was two more than she was used to. What she needed was some fresh air.

She headed for the fire stairs. At least it would be cool out there. Mumbling excuses as she bumped into people, stifling a cry as a heavy male shoe came down on her bare instep, she picked her way through the crowd, so absorbed in keeping her footing that she didn't notice Morgan Latimer standing by the fire door, blocking her way, until she almost ran into him.

After those first few brief glimpses of him, she'd only seen the back of his head occasionally, always in a group, and usually surrounded by a bevy of admiring women. Yet every once in a while she could have sworn he was watching her, and, now that they had come face-to-face, she wasn't really surprised.

She gave him a cool smile, and had just opened her mouth to say hello, when he forestalled her by holding out a hand.

"Good evening," he said. "I'm Morgan Latimer."

Once again he hadn't even recognized her! Nora was about to remind him that they'd already met, under not very auspicious circumstances, when she noticed the expression on his face, the way his eyes were raking her up and down, frankly admiring, even leering in a dignified sort of way, and a wild idea formed in her mind.

"How do you do," she murmured.

She let him take her hand. His skin was warm and dry, the touch electric, and she quickly drew it away.

"Well," he said. "Aren't you going to tell me your name?"

She had to say something. Stalling for time, she set her empty wineglass down on a nearby table, her mind racing, trying to come up with a clever reply. Finally, she turned back to him.

"But we've already met," she said, with what she hoped was an enigmatic smile.

He grinned, revealing even white teeth that dazzled against his tanned face, and shook his head vigorously. "No," he stated, in a positive tone. "We couldn't have. I'd never have forgotten you."

"Oh, but I'm afraid you must have." She pursed her lips in a slight pout. "Not very flattering, Mr. Latimer."

"Morgan, please."

"Well, Morgan, I was just about to get some fresh air. If you'd excuse me?" She started to brush past him, but he placed a hand lightly on her bare arm, holding her back.

"Not so fast," he said. "You've aroused my curiosity now, and I won't rest until it's satisfied." He smiled. "And I think you'll find I don't give up easily."

I'll just bet you don't, she thought. "Well, Morgan," she drawled seductively. "Neither do I."

He moved a step nearer, snaked an arm around her waist, and bent his head down close to hers. "Come on, mystery lady. Put me out of my misery. Who are you?"

She looked directly up into the gray eyes, the little black flecks glittering there, and a heady sense of power seized hold of her, making her reckless. *She* was in control here for a change! There was a hungry look in those eyes that *she* had put there! Drab little Nora Graham!

She batted her eyelashes at him. "I think I'll make you guess."

"A model," he said promptly. Then he raised his head and swept an appraising glance over her. "No, an actress." He frowned. "No, that doesn't quite fit, either. Are you? An actress?"

She shook her head, and gazed up at him, one eyebrow arched provocatively. "Not even close. Now, if you'll excuse me, I really do need some fresh air."

He stared at her for a long moment, as though debating whether to persist or give in. Then, suddenly, he inclined his head in an almost formal bow of acquiescence, and stepped aside.

She turned from him, opened the fire door and walked through, her head held high, not even glancing his way. When she heard the door clang behind her, shutting him out, she stumbled unsteadily over to the top of the staircase. Slowly, she walked down the concrete steps to the next landing, then stopped, leaned against the metal railing, and took several deep breaths of the cool air.

By now her knees were wobbly, her hands shaking, and her head whirling around. Although she felt she'd come out of the encounter quite well, she wasn't used to the stresses and strains of that kind of parlour game. She'd also had too much to drink, and was feeling the effects of it. But she had won a kind of victory, after all. She'd kept *him* guessing, for a change, given him a lesson in one-upmanship he wasn't likely to forget.

Now, as her head began to clear, the one thought in her mind was to get out of there without running into Morgan Latimer again. It was one thing to indulge in a game of verbal sparring with him and win at a party, decked out in her "disguise," but no victory was worth the Latimer account.

Even though his ego probably needed taking down a peg or two, she could well imagine how angry he would be if he found out who she really was, and that he'd been gulled by a flunkey whose livelihood virtually depended on *his* money. Her dreams of glory over the success of the ad campaign would be shattered irrevocably.

Now she was in a real panic. She'd have to go back inside, find Jerry, and talk him into leaving. If she couldn't pry him away from his redhead she'd get a taxi and go home alone. In the meantime, she'd just have to pray she didn't run into Morgan again.

She went back up the stairs and opened the fire door a crack, peering through it to see if he was anywhere around. There was no sign of him, and she quickly slipped through the door, searching the crowd for Jerry. Finally, she spotted his auburn hair, and made a beeline toward it.

But before she'd gone three steps, she came face-to-face with her boss, Robert McKenzie, bearing down on her, a man and woman with him whom she didn't know.

"Ah, there you are, Nora," he said. "I've been looking all over for you." He gave her a swift appraising glance. "You're looking very lovely tonight, by the way. Didn't know you had it in you." He turned to his companions. "I'd like you to meet Nora Graham, the guiding light behind the Latimer ad. Nora, this is Owen Latimer and his sister, Anne. Owen is the creative genius behind Latimer's, the man who designs all those marvelous clothes, and Anne supervises the cutting room."

Nora murmured a greeting, and shook hands with the Latimers. There wasn't a trace of Morgan's startling colouring, good looks or commanding presence in either one of them. They were both fair, rather pallid-looking people. The only similarity was in the eyes, the same silvery gray with the darker flecks, but softer than Morgan's, more kindly, less arrogant and challenging.

They were both smiling at her now, congratulating her on the success of her ad. Nora tried to pay attention, thanking them when it seemed appropriate, smiling distractedly, but she hardly heard a word they were saying. All she had on her mind was getting out of there, and the minute there was a lull in the conversation, she excused herself and started to leave to look for Jerry again.

But she was too late. Before she could take a step, Morgan suddenly appeared behind his brother and was gazing down at her with a smug, self-satisfied expression on his lean face. Aha! he seemed to be saying. I've caught you now.

"Bob," he said to McKenzie, "will you introduce me to your beautiful young friend?"

The older man stared at Morgan for a second, then broke into loud laughter. "Why, you and Nora met two months ago. Don't tell me you've forgotten! You probably didn't recognize her outside the office, in all her party finery."

A sudden light dawned in Morgan's eyes, and he reared his head back, an expression of stunned astonishment on his face. But he recovered quickly. A grim look settled around his mouth, and he glared at her balefully for a few seconds.

"Yes," he said at last, "of course." He turned to his brother. "Owen, this is the young lady who ordered me to take my clothes off the first time we met."

Four pairs of eyes, full of amusement, were gazing at her now. Nora flushed hot, then went cold, wishing she were anywhere in the world but in that place at that time. She was about to stammer out yet another explanation of that comedy of errors to the others, but by then a small knot of anger had begun to build just behind her eyes. Hadn't he beaten that humiliating story to death long ago? She'd be damned if she'd explain. Let them think what they liked.

She managed to force out a smile. "Such are the fortunes of war," she said pleasantly. "Now, I really must be going. Thank you very much for inviting me to the party, Miss Latimer. It was lovely."

"I'll take you home," Morgan announced, in a positive tone.

"No, thank you," Nora stated, equally positive. "I came with someone else."

By now he had crossed to her side, and had taken her by the arm. "If you mean the photographer, he's long gone."

"Then I'll find my own way..." she began, but the grip on her arm suddenly tightened, and, before she knew what was happening, he was already steering her through the crowd toward the main entrance. "Ouch!" she said, glaring up at him. "That hurts."

"Good," he muttered through his teeth. "I ought to wring your neck."

Short of sitting down on the floor and refusing to budge, there wasn't much Nora could do at this point. This maniac at her side was perfectly capable of creating a scene if she resisted him. He seemed to be wound up tighter than a drum, and the tension in the hand gripping her so tightly was palpable. Besides, if Jerry had left with his redhead, she'd have to find her own way home, anyway.

"You don't have to break my arm," she said, as they approached the bank of elevators. "I'll go quietly."

He didn't release his hold on her until the doors were closed behind them and they were on their way down, nor did he utter one word until they stepped out into the deserted lobby of the building. They walked silently together to the entrance, out into the street, then down a block to where a sleek gray Mercedes was parked.

He unlocked the door and held it open while she got inside. While he went around to the driver's side, she sat there shivering, wondering what was ahead. She didn't believe for a moment he would actually do her bodily harm, and it was actually too late to fire her now that the ad had been such a success. As a matter of fact, she wasn't in the least worried about her job. Even though Latimer's was a huge account, it wasn't the only one in New York. If the worse came to the worst, the agency would survive without it.

What she was afraid of, however, was a scene. Raised by loving parents in a small town where everyone knew everybody else, four pleasant uneventful years in a small college with no violent upheavals, and sliding rather smoothly into a job she was good at, she'd had very little experience with downright hostility.

Of course you couldn't live one day in Manhattan without being snarled at by a salesperson, or almost run down by an irate taxi driver, but she'd soon learnt that it was just the New York way, that underneath the contentious exterior these individuals were just as vulnerable, just as kindhearted and friendly as the people she'd known back in Wimslow.

Morgan was inside the car now, the door slammed behind him. After a while, when he made no motion to start the engine, she gave him a swift sideways glance. His hands were gripping the steering wheel, and he was staring straight ahead. In the glow of the streetlight overhead, she could just make out his grim expression.

Finally, he turned to her. "All right, Miss Graham. Would you care to explain that little charade back there?"

She shrugged. "I was just having a little fun with you."

He cocked an eyebrow at her. "You mean you were enjoying yourself at my expense."

Suddenly, all Nora's apprehension simply vanished. There was nothing this man could do to her. She'd made a fool of him and he didn't like it, but that was just too bad. She shifted in her seat so that her back was resting against the door, folded her arms across her chest, and gave him a long, direct look.

"Listen," she said. "You'll have to admit that you've had a lot of mileage out of that stupid story about my telling you to take your clothes off. I don't see where you have any right to complain because I pulled a fast one on you and got a little of my own back. And after all, we *had* met before. I wasn't lying to you. You just didn't remember me."

He stared at her for a moment, his face expressionless. "Well, I'm not apt to forget you again, am I?" Then, abruptly, he turned from her, and started the car. "Where to?" he asked, as they pulled out into the late-night traffic.

She gave him her address, and they drove the entire way to her place in silence. Actually, she was quite proud of herself for standing up to him the way she had. Let him sulk, if it made him happy. Until he came along, it had actually been quite a successful party, after all—the heavy investment in clothes and coiffure, manicure and makeup worth every penny. She'd been the center of a lot of admiring male attention, and had enjoyed it immensely.

In front of her building, he pulled up at the curb, and shut off the engine. Nora reached for the door handle. "Thank you for the lift," she said stiffly, and started to get out.

"When I called you several weeks ago," he said, "why wouldn't you go out with me?"

Nora turned around and stared at him, amazed that he'd even remembered he had called her. She'd almost forgotten it herself. "I told you," she said. "I'd promised my parents I'd go home that weekend."

"And that's what you did?"

"Of course."

"You weren't playing games?"

She laughed shortly. "I wouldn't even know how. Tonight was my first attempt."

He turned to her and smiled. "And a very successful one, too." He cocked his head to one side. "That was quite a crowd you had gathered around you back there. And I had the feeling it wasn't because you happen to be so good at your job."

The smile utterly transformed him. And he *had* noticed her! But why was he turning on the charm now? Could he be looking for a way to get back at her? No, he might have been annoyed at her little deception tonight, but he wasn't the kind to hold a grudge. She meant nothing to him, after all. Even if she had wounded his ego slightly, he had his pick of beautiful women who would be only too happy to stroke it.

"I guess I should apologize," she said. "But when you didn't even recognize me, I simply couldn't resist."

"Then we're even?"

She nodded. "Entirely quits."

"Good. Then have dinner with me tomorrow night."

Her mouth fell open. "Are you serious?"

"I'm always serious," he announced.

"I'm sorry. I can't tomorrow night."

"How about Monday, then? Or Tuesday; you name the day. This time I'm not going to let you slip away."

Nora's heart was pounding, her mind in a whirl. Instead of dumping her on the pavement in a rage, here he was pursuing her with a determination she couldn't resist. All because she'd bought a new dress? Well, if that's what it took to attract a man like Morgan Latimer, that's what she'd do. It was worth every penny.

Still, she couldn't quite beat down a little warning voice that told her this man was dangerous, that getting involved with him would be like playing with fire. But one dinner date was hardly an 'involvement.' Besides, she'd never forgive herself if

she missed an opportunity like this one out of
cowardice.

"All right," she said at last. "Monday."

"Good. I'll pick you up here at your place at
seven o'clock."

He came around to open her door, helped her
out, and walked with her to the entrance of her
building. When she'd unlocked the door and he'd
seen her safely inside, he said good-night, and left.

Nora stumbled into her apartment, still in a daze,
but filled with a heady sense of wild elation. She
was going to have an adventure! And the first step
was to go back to that wonderful wardrobe consultant and choose some new clothes.

Jerry called late the next morning, abjectly apologetic, and obviously badly hung over.

"Hi, Nora," he said, in a subdued, cautious tone.
"It's Jerry."

"Well, good morning," she replied. "What happened to you last night?"

"Uh, listen, Nora, I'm really sorry about that.
I just got carried away. You see, there was this
girl..."

He went on in that vein for a few minutes, and
as she listened to the thick halting voice Nora's
amusement grew with each passing moment. She
was still in her bathrobe and slippers, sitting by the
telephone in the small foyer of her flat, munching
the last of her breakfast toast, and sipping coffee.

Finally, when he'd come to the end of his involved explanations, his voice trailing off limply,
Nora swallowed the last bite of toast and exploded
into the laughter she could no longer contain.

"Ouch!" Jerry protested. "Don't do that!"

"Don't do what?"

"Laugh in my ear like that. You're talking to a sick man."

"Hah! You're just hung over."

"Believe me, that's a real sickness," was the fervent heartfelt reply. He paused for a moment, then went on in a cautious tone, "Then you're not mad?"

"I should be," she retorted sharply. "But no, you're forgiven. I just hope that redhead was worth it."

"I don't kiss and tell," he replied, in a prim voice. "Besides, you weren't doing badly yourself. I never would have left you in the lurch like that if you hadn't had ten guys hanging around making eyes at you."

"That's a slight exaggeration," she said dryly.

"Oh, yeah? The last time I saw you Morgan Latimer was practically eating out of your hand. So how did you get home? Did Latimer take you?"

Nora hesitated. For some reason, she wanted to keep her memory of last night to herself. She still hadn't quite thought it through, what she hoped for from the relationship, what she could expect—most of all, what she feared.

"Well, yes, he did give me a lift home—out of the kindness of his heart, I might add, seeing that my escort had abandoned me."

"Come on, Nora, don't make me feel worse than I already do. I apologized very nicely, and you said I was forgiven."

Having successfully sidetracked him from the subject of Morgan Latimer, Nora was prepared to be generous. "Sorry," she said, "I couldn't resist."

"So go on, tell me what happened," he persisted. "Did you have to beat him off? Are you going to see him again?"

Nora sighed. Obviously, Jerry wasn't going to be led off the scent so easily. "As a matter of fact, I am," she said.

"You mean you're going out with him?"

"Yes. I'm having dinner with him tomorrow night. But, Jerry, please keep it to yourself. I don't want it spread all over the office."

"Yeah, sure," he replied. He paused for a few seconds, then went on in a dead serious tone, "Listen, Nora, I don't mean to interfere in your personal life, but I just hope you know what you're doing. I mean, the guy has a reputation that's legendary around town. He eats little girls like you for breakfast."

"It's only a dinner date, Jerry," she insisted, with elaborate patience. "Besides, I'm a big girl. I can take care of myself."

"Sure," he agreed swiftly. "Sorry. I didn't mean to butt in. Well, if I'm really forgiven, I think a couple of aspirin and the rest of the day in bed are next on my agenda."

After she hung up the telephone, Nora walked slowly back to the kitchen for another cup of coffee, frowning as she went. Somehow, telling Jerry about her date with Morgan, and listening to him voice those dire warnings, seemed to take some of the joy out of it. Was she letting herself in for more than she could handle? Probably, she had to admit. But there was no way she was going to back out now.

The next night the doorbell rang promptly at seven o'clock. Before answering it, Nora took one more look at herself in the bathroom mirror. She'd left work early that afternoon to have her hair done and shop for a new dress, but hadn't had time for a professional makeup job and had had to do it herself.

Now, as she peered closely at her reflection, it didn't look quite right. The pale blue eyeshadow looked too garish for the neat black dress she'd chosen, the blusher seemed to glow on her cheeks in two circles, and she'd dripped mascara on her right eyelid. She'd been nervous enough to begin with. Now she began to panic. She'd just have to wash her face and start all over again.

The doorbell rang again, this time with a note of impatience. She didn't have time. She couldn't keep him standing out there on the doorstep while she completely remade her face. She grabbed a tissue and scrubbed at her cheeks until the blusher blended more subtly, then wet the tissue and dabbed the dots of mascara away, removing some of the eyeshadow in the process.

She smoothed down the slim skirt of her new dress. At least that looked all right. It was one of those sedate little dresses that seemed to cover everything but fitted so well that the figure underneath it was clearly revealed. She'd had her hair done in the same elaborate style she'd worn at the party on Saturday, and the combination of svelte dress and sleek coiffure made her look quite sophisticated, even glamorous. If the makeup wasn't quite right, the lights would probably be dim wherever they went.

The only problem was, she thought, just before she switched off the light over the mirror, she didn't look in the least like herself. But she did look like the kind of woman Morgan would be glad to be seen with, and that's what counted at the moment.

When she opened the door, her heart still pounding, her knees knocking, her nervousness vanished the moment she saw the frankly appreciative glint in his gray eyes. She was an attractive woman about to go out on the town in one of the most exciting cities in the world with a devastating man. What more could a girl want?

CHAPTER FOUR

"COME in," she said. "I'll just get my coat and bag."

As he stepped inside and shut the door behind him, he seemed to fill the small room. He stood there in the shadows, his tall form outlined against the door, his arms folded across his chest, his slightly hooded eyes sweeping her up and down.

"You look as though you've just stepped out of a fashion magazine yourself," he said at last. He laughed shortly. "It's no wonder I didn't recognize you at the party."

Nora smiled uncertainly. He was so tall! And he looked absolutely marvelous, his crisp dark hair neatly brushed, his lean cheeks freshly shaven, his white teeth gleaming against his tan. It was no wonder she'd mistaken him for a model, considering the way the dark suit hung on his lean frame so perfectly.

He came a few steps closer to her so that his face was in the light. "What happened to the Nora Graham I met a few months ago?"

Was there a hint of regret in his voice? Disappointment? Surely not. There was no comparison between the image she projected tonight, which surely was exactly what attracted a man like Morgan, and the frowsy, harried person she'd been when they first met, in her shapeless suit, her hair pinned up so carelessly, her face totally innocent of makeup.

She shrugged. "I don't know. I guess I just decided I needed a change."

His smile broadened, and he moved another step nearer. "Well, I must say I heartily approve. I've been wondering ever since I took you home from the party the other night why in the world I let you slip away when you couldn't make it for dinner that time."

She laughed. "I'm sure you had other more interesting things on your mind."

"Actually, I had to leave for Paris the next day, and was gone for three weeks." He shook his head. "Well, it doesn't matter now, does it? All's well that ends well. Shall we go?"

Something about his explanation didn't ring quite true to her, and, during the short taxi ride to the restaurant, she had to wonder what he wasn't telling her. He probably had left town the following day, as he'd said, but that didn't explain why he hadn't called her when he came back. It could only be one thing. He'd undoubtedly had other more interesting feminine fish to fry.

However, he was right. At this point, it didn't really matter. Best to put the whole episode out of her mind, and enjoy the evening.

At the restaurant, one of the most exclusive—and expensive—in the city, he was greeted by the headwaiter like a long-lost friend, fawned over and catered to as though he were an Eastern potentate who had descended on them. They were given one of the best tables by the dance floor, where a small orchestra was playing show tunes.

"Will you have a drink?" he asked, when they were seated.

"Yes, please. A dry sherry, I think."

While Morgan ordered their drinks from the hovering cocktail waiter, Nora leaned back in her chair, and gazed around the crowded room. Even in the dim light, she'd already recognized an important gossip columnist, a famous actress, and a talk-show host.

When their drinks arrived, Morgan raised his glass. "What shall we drink to?" he asked.

"Oh, the success of the Latimer ad campaign, of course," she replied. "What else?"

"Oh, I can think of a few things. But that'll do."

"Speaking of Latimer's," she said, "I didn't realize it was such a family affair until I met your brother and sister at the party. You must get along well to have been in business together for so long."

He laughed. "Oh, we have our disagreements. Owen is rather a temperamental type, and Anne and I have to sit on some of his more outrageous ideas once in a while. He's invaluable, of course, as the creative mind behind our designs, but when he wanders into the world of business he's like a child."

"And that's your bailiwick," she said. "The business end."

He nodded. "Yes, but Anne is an enormous help. Of course, now that she has a family, she's not as active as she used to be. I do most of the traveling."

"I envy you. I've never been anywhere."

He raised an eyebrow. "Oh? Well, perhaps one day you will."

The waiter brought the menus to them, and while they finished their drinks they debated what to have for dinner. Everything was in French, with no prices, and Nora had no idea what to order. Her college French course had been long forgotten. Finally, she set the menu down, and looked at Morgan.

"I can't decide. Will you order for me?"

"All right. Although I usually just have a steak."

"That sounds perfect," she agreed promptly.

He glanced at her empty wine glass. "How about another drink while we wait for the food?"

She nodded, and he raised a hand for the cocktail waiter, who appeared immediately. While Morgan ordered their drinks, Nora debated whether to pursue the subject of his family. As she was an only child, other people's brothers and sisters fascinated her. He didn't seem to mind talking about them.

"You mentioned that your sister had a family," she said, when the second round of drinks arrived. "I take it that means a husband and children."

"Yes," he replied. "Definitely a husband, who is the lawyer for Latimer's, and four children at last count."

"How about your brother, Owen?"

"No, Owen and I think pretty much along the same lines on that subject."

"Meaning?"

To her amazement, a dull flush washed over his face. His jaw clamped shut, and his eyes narrowed. "Meaning that we both have seen all we need to of family life to convince us that it's not for us."

The bitterness in his voice was unmistakable. She'd obviously touched on forbidden territory. But how was she to know? Although she was sorry she'd trodden on a tender spot, she had the feeling that his irritation was not so much directed at her for asking the question as it was a cover-up for a still-raw wound. This intrigued her, made him seem more human, but he'd made it clear that the subject was definitely out of bounds.

She stared down at her wineglass, twirling it around in slow circles on the heavy white cloth, wondering if an apology was in order, trying to dream up a neutral topic of conversation that would breach the awkward moment.

Finally, she just decided to make an inane comment about the weather, but when she glanced across the table at him he was smiling at her, leaning back in his chair, once again totally at ease, the incident apparently forgotten.

"That's a very dull subject," he said, with an easy offhand gesture. He put his elbows on the table, hands laced under his chin, and leaned toward her. "What fascinates me is how a woman as lovely as you can also manage to be so competent in her profession."

Nora wasn't used to that kind of flattery, and she was taken aback, uncertain how to respond to it. "I don't know about that," she murmured non-committally.

"Well, take my word for it," he said easily. "It's no wonder I didn't recognize you. I've never seen such a transformation. What brought about the new Nora? I rather liked the old one."

She laughed. "But not enough even to recognize her the next time you saw her."

He creased his forehead in a puzzled expression. "You mean at the party?"

"No. Before that. We ran into each other at the agency. You were waiting for the elevator when I came out of it."

He shook his head. "Sorry. I don't remember that."

She laughed. "Well, I can hardly blame you. It was pouring down with rain outside that day, and I was drenched."

He leaned even closer toward her, his eyes narrowed at her, a crooked smile on his lips. "Well, I'm not likely to forget you again."

Just then the orchestra came back from their break, and started playing. "My one objection to this place," he said, "is that the service is rather slow. We have plenty of time. Would you care to dance?"

"Yes," she said. "I'd like that."

They got up from their chairs, and walked together toward the floor, where three or four other couples had already started to dance. When they reached it, he turned to her, and, after just a second's hesitation, she moved into his waiting arms.

He was a wonderful dancer, smooth and light on his feet for such a big man. He held her loosely at first, but before long the arm around her waist tightened, pulling her body slowly but inexorably close up against his.

As she drifted along in his arms, light as a feather, a slow warmth began to steal through her. His cheek was pressed against hers now, slightly rough and rasping, and she breathed in his clean musky scent.

With each step he took the electricity between them seemed to crackle as thigh brushed against thigh.

When the dance was over, they stood in a dim corner of the floor, not moving, his arms still around her. Still reeling, she looked up into his face, and what she saw there took her breath away. The gray eyes were gleaming, hungry, devouring her, but there was something else. She tried to warn herself that this man was a practiced seducer, that he had one thing on his mind, that she was being swept off her feet by a man far wiser in the ways of love than anyone she'd ever known.

But it was too late. She might be playing with fire, but she was so far in over her head by now that she didn't care. In her heart of hearts, she knew that whatever it was this man wanted of her she was probably going to give it to him eventually.

Back at the table, the wine steward appeared, and while he and Morgan discussed vintages Nora gazed happily around the elegant dining room. She felt as though she were floating on a cloud, like Cinderella at the ball, the handsome prince sitting across from her.

The new image had worked better than she ever would have dreamed. He'd said he rather liked the old Nora, but that wasn't the Nora he'd gone out of his way to pursue, to flatter, to please. Now that she'd transformed herself, she had him eating out of her hand. Well, not quite, but it looked promising.

Just then, she noticed a familiar-looking man making his way toward them. She knew she'd seen him before, but couldn't quite place him until he stood beside their table, staring down at them with a broad grin, and an odd knowing glint in his eye. Then she recognized him as Ralph Corbett, a prominent society reporter for one of the major daily newspapers.

"Good evening, Mr. Latimer," he said, in an unctuous voice that virtually oozed out of him. His eyes darted at Nora. "Mind if I ask who the lovely young lady is?"

"Now, Corbett," Morgan drawled easily, "you know better than to ask me that." He was smiling, but there was an undercurrent of steel in his voice. "I'll talk about business any time you like, but my personal life is my own affair."

"Ah, but you're a public figure, Mr. Latimer," Corbett persisted. "And public figures have no personal life. Come on," he wheedled. "I'll find out, anyway. Might as well get the straight story from you."

Morgan sighed. He gave Nora a quick glance, his eyebrows lifted in a question. She didn't know what to do, how to respond, so she merely shrugged.

"All right, Corbett," Morgan said to the reporter, in a clipped, brusque voice. "Her name is Nora Graham. She's with the McKenzie-Phillips advertising agency that handles the Latimer account."

"Then are you saying this is a business dinner?" the reporter asked, in a deceptively innocent tone. Nora could virtually see the tongue in his cheek. Corbett gave her an openly suggestive leer. "That hardly does justice to the lady's obvious charms."

"That's all I have to say," Morgan announced flatly.

The reporter nodded, turned and walked off. Nora sat there, watching him go, her cheeks burning. Somehow the episode had cast a slight pall on the enchanting evening. The implication of that last look he'd given her had been crystal clear. She would most likely appear in his column tomorrow as just one more of Morgan Latimer's conquests.

Well, what had she expected? She looked at Morgan, who was sitting back in his chair, a cigarette in one hand, his drink in the other, gazing around the room with a bemused expression, just as though nothing out of the way had happened. To him, it probably hadn't.

However, he glanced her way, and his face sobered instantly. "You mustn't let Corbett disturb you, Nora," he said. He reached across the table, and put a hand over hers. "He's just one of the vultures who feed on prominent people whose names happen to make society news."

The touch of his hand on hers, large and warm, seemed to reassure her. She gave him an uncertain smile. He squeezed her hand, and the pressure sent a tingling sensation up her arm that convinced her she was being silly to worry about such things. After all, if she was going to play in the big leagues, she'd have to expect to go by the rules. It didn't seem to bother Morgan. He'd handled the reporter quite masterfully. There was nothing to be concerned about.

Their steaks arrived, and while they ate they chatted easily, mostly about Nora. He had a way of leading her into discussions of her family, her life at school, her work, even her personal life, that made her feel he considered her the most interesting person he'd ever met, and her rather dull past a fascinating saga of success won over enormous odds.

Every once in a while, conscious that she was babbling on about herself in a way she'd never done before, she tried to steer the conversation towards his own background and personal experience, but each time he would deftly sidestep her questions, not exactly refusing to answer, but waving them aside as though his history was of no consequence.

"How about some dessert?" he asked, when she'd finished the last bite of perfectly broiled steak.

"Oh, I couldn't," she said with a groan. "It was wonderful, but I'm stuffed."

"Well, then, an after-dinner drink?"

"No, thanks." She sighed. "I'd like to just sit here and digest for a while. But you go ahead if you like."

"No. I think I'll pass, too."

They sat there in an easy silence for a while, listening to the music, watching the dancers. Nora felt as though she were in seventh heaven, floating in a bubble, riding high on a cloud. For the first time in her life, a devastating man was treating her like a desirable woman, and she never wanted it to end. The unpleasantness with the reporter and the way Morgan had reacted to her personal questions still hovered at the edges of her consciousness, threatening to disturb her euphoric glow, but she quickly closed her mind to them whenever they appeared. *Nothing* was going to spoil this lovely evening for her.

"Tell me," he said at last. "What are your future plans? I mean, professionally."

"Well, I'm not sure. I guess I haven't really thought about it much. I love my job, and it seems to be working out well for me." She smiled. "So I guess my plans are to keep doing it as well as I can, and hope for the best."

"And what is the best? I mean, surely, as a dedicated professional, you must have some ultimate goal in mind. For example, what would be your wildest dream?"

She laughed. "I don't know."

She rested an elbow on the table and put her chin in her hand, thinking hard. His question seemed to be aimed entirely at her professional life, and she had to ask herself whether her wildest dreams actually were centered around her work. What about marriage, children, a home, and family of her own? Weren't they part of it?

But that hadn't been what he'd asked her. "I suppose," she said slowly at last, "that my wildest dream would be to become a partner in the McKenzie firm."

He nodded then, and gave her an encouraging smile of satisfaction, as though she'd just passed a test of some kind. Then, the gray eyes glinting, he reached out a hand and put it on her bare forearm, his long fingers moving slowly, caressingly, up and down, then making a circle around her wrist.

"I can help you make that dream come true," he said, in a low voice.

Nora stared at him, totally taken off balance. Then she stiffened, suddenly alert. Did he mean what she thought he meant? Suddenly the lovely evening, the pleasant glow, began to fade into a tarnished image, cheap and so utterly predictable that it was almost funny. She left her arm where it was, under the pressure of those stroking fingers, but the magic was gone.

"I'm not sure what you mean," she said, and was surprised at how steady her voice sounded, considering the turmoil underneath.

He shrugged. "Well, for one thing, the Latimer account is entirely a feather in your own cap, after all. No one gave it to you. You earned it yourself. I'm talking about the future."

"What about the future?"

He withdrew his hand and pushed his chair back. "Shall we leave now?" he asked smoothly. "We can discuss it further in a less public place. Perhaps at your place. Or mine, if you'd care to see where I live."

Nora almost laughed out loud at the tired, over-worked old question. Your place or mine! Couldn't he even come up with something a little more original than that?

She searched her mind for a way to respond. What she wanted to do at this point was to slap that clever knowing look off his face, stalk out of the restaurant, and find her own way home. But something held her back. Maybe it was the fact that he was a major client of the firm. Maybe it was a lingering hope that she was mistaken. At any rate, she knew she had to find out for sure before she did or said anything she might be sorry for later.

"Actually, I think I would like that drink after all," she said quickly.

He raised one inquiring eyebrow, then settled down in his chair again, and raised a hand for the cocktail waiter, who came scurrying to the table as though he'd been hovering in the wings just waiting for a summons to make his entrance onstage.

"I'll have a brandy," Morgan said to him. "Nora? What would you like?"

"Uh, brandy will be fine." Since she was only stalling for time, and had no intention of drinking any more, it didn't matter.

"Would you like to dance again while we're waiting?" he asked.

"No. No, thank you. I don't think so." It was the last thing she wanted. Once she was in his arms again, she'd be lost, and she needed a clear head.

Their drinks arrived almost immediately, and after one token sip Nora leaned back in her chair, trying to look relaxed and casual. "Could you spell out in a little more detail what you had in mind when you said you could help me with my career?" she asked, in a careful, neutral tone of voice.

He frowned. "Did it really sound as crass as all that? I didn't mean it in that way. At least, not exactly."

Nora took another sip of the brandy she hadn't intended to drink at all, and as the fiery liquid coursed through her bloodstream, warming her, she suddenly became thoroughly fed up with all this sparring around.

"Let me guess, then," she said quite calmly. "If I read you right, what you're suggesting is that you will use your influence, your clout, with my employers to give my dream of a partnership a boost if I'll go to bed with you."

To her intense delight, he seemed at a total loss for words. His eyes widened, he opened his mouth, then snapped it shut again, then glared at her. "That's a rather crude way of putting it."

"But that's pretty much what you meant, isn't it?"

She held him in her gaze, waiting. When he dropped his eyes, she knew she'd been right. There was no point in further discussion. She knew what she had to do. Quickly, she pushed her chair back, gathered up the stole she'd draped over the back of it, and reached for her handbag. Then she rose to her feet, and stood looking down at him.

"Sorry, Mr. Latimer," she said, in a low, firm voice. "I'm not interested. My job means a lot to me, but it doesn't mean everything." She threw one end of the stole over her shoulder in a sweeping gesture. "Thanks for the dinner, but I'll find my own way home."

She turned and walked off, her head held high, praying she wouldn't trip or bump into someone on the way to mar her dramatic exit.

By the time she'd made it out to the street, her whole body was shaking, and her knees had begun to buckle. Frantically, she hailed a cab, and scurried inside the minute it pulled up, as if afraid Morgan might come running out to catch her. Once they'd pulled safely away from the curb, she leaned her head back on the seat, and closed her eyes.

Although her heart was still pounding, she felt an enormous sense of satisfaction at what she'd just done. Of course there might be unpleasant consequences. Morgan Latimer wielded a lot of power in her world, and if he really wanted to seek revenge her career could very well be at an end.

Somehow, however, it didn't seem to matter quite as much as it once did.

His questions tonight about her goals, her wildest dreams, had made her stop and think what it was she really wanted. She'd even been a little disappointed that he so obviously meant it in a professional sense. *Was* a partnership in McKenzie-Phillips the be-all and end-all of her existence? She thought about her parents, the solidity and content of their married life, marred only by the fact that no more children had come after she was born.

But times had changed since then. Nora's generation of women was no longer content to stay at home and spend their lives producing babies, making a comfortable haven for men. She loved her job, knew she was good at it, and even if Morgan Latimer drove her out of New York his power didn't encompass the whole world!

When the taxi driver pulled up in front of her building, she paid him, and hurried up the stairs to her apartment, where she immediately stripped off the new black dress, scrubbed her face, and got into her pajamas. It wasn't very late, only ten o'clock, but it had been an exhausting evening, and tomorrow was a working day.

It wasn't until she was safely in her own bed, alone, the lights turned out, the noises of the city drifting in through the half-open window, that it struck her. What in the world had possessed Morgan to make that silly suggestion about helping her with her career in the first place? A man that attractive surely didn't have to buy his women!

* * *

The next morning Nora had just hung up her coat and settled herself at her desk when Gloria burst into the office, her face flushed with excitement and waving aloft in one hand a copy of the morning newspaper.

"Nora!" she cried. "You're famous!"

"What in the world are you talking about?" Nora asked, bewildered.

Gloria slapped the paper down on the desk, and pointed to the middle of the page. "Just read that. Ralph Corbett's column."

Nora glanced down at Corbett's photograph. Beneath it, in the first paragraph, she immediately spotted her own name. She glanced quickly up at Gloria, who stood there beaming, just as though her favorite child had won a coveted award.

"Go on," she said. "Read it." Then, when Nora continued to stare blankly at her, she snatched up the pages again with a snort of impatience. "Here, I'll read it to you." She cleared her throat.

"Morgan Latimer, one of Manhattan's most eligible and elusive bachelors, has displayed his discriminating taste in women once again by squiring around the beautiful Nora Graham. Ms. Graham, one of the brighter—and most decorative—young stars at the McKenzie-Phillips advertising agency, was the guiding light behind the recent Latimer ad campaign. Not to diminish the lady's ability, but being seen around with Morgan Latimer can't hurt a budding career.'

Nora's face was blazing before Gloria was even halfway through. It was exactly what she'd been afraid of when Corbett had come to the table last night. She glared at Gloria, who was still glowing, thrilled out of her mind by what she obviously considered a triumph for her boss.

"Well?" she said. "How about that?"

Nora got up from her chair, strode over to the window and stood staring out at the wall of the building next door. It was raining outside, great sheets of it slashing against the windowpane. She'd never felt so angry, so betrayed, so *cheap* in her life.

Slowly she turned around. "I think it's disgusting, that's what I think," she announced grimly.

Just then Jerry appeared in the doorway. He, too, was carrying a copy of the same newspaper, grinning broadly. He stopped just inside the door, and glanced from Nora to Gloria, the paper still in her hand, then back to Nora again.

"Uh, I take it you've already seen it," he said warily.

"If you'll excuse me . . ." Gloria said stiffly, and scurried past Jerry out into the hall.

When she was gone, Jerry closed the door, and took a few cautious steps toward Nora, who had remained at the window, her whole body rigid, her hands clenched into fists at her sides, her face still bright red.

"Now listen, Nora," Jerry began, "don't get upset at what one stupid columnist says . . ."

"It's not so much what he says," Nora erupted angrily. "It's what he implies."

Jerry shrugged. "Well, yeah, but no one pays any attention to that kind of gossip. He just wants to sell newspapers. Everyone understands that."

Nora went back to the desk, slumped down in her chair, and put her head in her hands. Now that the first furious reaction had dissipated and she'd cooled down a little, a sudden wave of desperation was beginning to descend on her.

After a while she raised her head and gazed up bleakly at Jerry. "The crazy thing is that it's partly true."

Jerry perched on the edge of the desk and gave her a disbelieving look. "Now, what's that supposed to mean? I know you better than to think you'd ever trade favors for a boost up in your career. In the first place, you don't need to. And in the second place, Morgan Latimer doesn't have to do that kind of thing to get all the women he wants."

"Well, that's what I thought, too. But, Jerry, he did make me a kind of proposition."

Jerry's eyes flew open. "You mean he actually came right out with it? I mean..." He waved a hand helplessly in the air. "Well, you know what I mean."

"Not exactly. But he certainly hinted at it."

Jerry shook his head. "I can't believe it. That's not his style."

"Well, then, what is his style?"

Jerry thought a minute. "Hell, I don't know. I guess I just assumed that a guy with his looks and charisma..." He stopped short and gave her a penetrating look. "What did you do when he made his hints?"

"I told him to forget it, in no uncertain terms, then got up from the table, and walked out."

Jerry slapped his knee and burst into loud peals of raucous laughter. "Oh, no, I wish I'd been there to see that!" He shook his head admiringly. "How did Latimer take it?"

"I haven't the slightest idea." She grinned sheepishly. "I didn't look back to check his reaction." Jerry's laughter had been just the antidote she needed. It *was* rather funny.

He glanced at his watch. "Uh-oh, I'd better take off. Got an early shooting schedule to make, and I'm already late." He slid off the desk, and stood looking down at her for a moment. "Listen, Nora, I wouldn't worry for a second about that item in Corbett's column. Anyone who knows you won't believe it, anyway. And no matter how mad you made Latimer, there really isn't much he can do to you. McKenzie will back you all the way."

"I hope you're right, Jerry."

"Oh, I am. You wait and see." He headed toward the door, and when he reached it he turned around, grinning. "But I wouldn't count on his calling and asking you out again in the near future."

With a little wave, he went out through the door. When he was gone, Nora stared down at the newspaper he'd left on her desk for a few minutes. Then, with an impatient gesture, she swept it up and threw it into the wastepaper basket.

She reached for the file on her latest project, a television commercial for a line of children's toys. She had to have it in the works in time for the Christmas season, and it was already October. Jerry's pep talk had done her a world of good, and she plunged into the world of dolls and trains with renewed vigor.

* * *

She worked steadily through the lunch hour, scribbling notes for Gloria to transcribe later, and making a final checklist for what still needed to be done, and finally, by one o'clock, her growling stomach told her it was time to stop.

Wearily, she flexed her aching fingers, and stretched her cramped shoulder muscles. She was exhausted, but satisfied with the morning's work. She rose to her feet and gathered up the file, ready to give it to Gloria to sort out later, when she looked up to see her assistant standing in the doorway.

One glance at Gloria's expressionless face and air of injured dignity told Nora that her feelings were still hurt by the way she'd reacted to the newspaper item Gloria had been so thrilled about. She'd have to make it up to her some way.

"Have you had lunch?" she asked. Gloria only shook her head. "Well," Nora went on, "let's have it together. My treat."

Gloria gave her a wary look. "I'm not very hungry."

"Listen, Gloria, I apologize for snapping at you that way this morning. I was just a little upset." She smiled. "Come on, don't be mad at me."

"Well . . ."

"Go on, get your coat. I'll just put this file away until we get back."

Just then the telephone on her desk rang and she leaned over to pick it up. "Nora Graham," she said.

"Hello, Nora. It's Morgan."

She almost dropped the receiver. His was the last voice she'd ever expected—or wanted—to hear again. She glanced at Gloria, still hesitating at the door, and covered the mouthpiece. "Go on. This will only take a second." When Gloria was gone, she'd had just enough time to recover.

"Yes," she said, in a clipped voice. "What can I do for you?"

"Well, first of all I want to apologize for any misunderstanding we might have had last night. I'm afraid I bungled it badly. Then, when I saw Corbett's column this morning, it only made matters worse." He paused, but when Nora didn't say anything he went on, "At any rate, I'd like a chance to make it up to you. Have dinner with me tonight."

CHAPTER FIVE

NORA sank down slowly into her chair. She'd expected trouble from him about her job, perhaps a furious confrontation at some point in the future, but for him to call her the day after she'd walked out on him in public left her utterly speechless.

"I'm sorry," she said at last. "I can't. And there's absolutely no need to make anything up to me. I admit I wasn't thrilled by that column, but I don't see that any real damage has been done. Anyway, thank you for calling. I have to go now. Goodbye."

"Hey, wait a minute!" he said. "Don't hang up. I said I was sorry."

"Yes, and I accept your apology. Now, unless you have business to discuss, I don't see that we have anything more to say to each other."

"That's a pretty hard-nosed line to take, isn't it?" he asked, in a pleasant, conversational tone. He chuckled. "After all, you walked out on me. Isn't that revenge enough?"

Nora sighed. "I don't want revenge."

"Then have dinner with me."

"No. I can't do that. I don't think it would be wise."

"Well, how about lunch then? Have you had lunch?"

"No," she replied slowly.

"My office isn't far away. We could meet in some out-of-the-way place where there won't be any reporters. You name it."

Did she dare? Her mind raced. Why not? He was the one who was being so insistent. "All right," she said at last. "I'll meet you in ten minutes at Schrafft's on the corner."

"Good. I'll be there."

When they'd hung up Nora sat there for a moment, grinning wickedly. In a few minutes Gloria appeared at the door, carrying her coat. "What's got into you?" she asked. "You look like the cat who's swallowed the canary."

"Maybe I have." Nora stood up, and went over to get her coat. "I'll tell you about it on the way, so you won't faint dead away when he shows up."

Gloria was still giggling nervously when they were seated in the back booth of the restaurant. At first she'd demurred, claiming she didn't want to have any part in embarrassing such an important client, but Nora had insisted.

"Listen, you've got to come along. I wouldn't have agreed to meet him if I hadn't known you were going to be there. What harm can it do?"

Finally, Gloria had agreed, and by now was even beginning to show some enthusiasm. "I can hardly wait to see his face," she said excitedly.

He'd said ten minutes, but when the busy waitress finally arrived at their booth to take their order they'd already been there over twenty.

"We might as well order," Nora said. "He may have decided not to come at all."

They were halfway through their lunch when he did show up. Nora spotted him the moment he came inside, and watched him as he stood in the entrance for a moment, scanning the room. He was wearing the same light gray trenchcoat he'd had on that day she'd run into him at the elevators. It was unbelted, hanging loosely over a darker gray suit. When he finally saw her, he made straight for the booth, smiling broadly.

"So you did come," he said. "Sorry I'm a little late, but an unexpected problem came up at the office." Then he noticed Gloria, who was gazing up at him raptly, with innocent brown eyes, and he turned to Nora with a mildly questioning look.

"This is Gloria Salerno, my assistant," Nora said, with a perfectly straight face. "I believe you've already met."

"Ah, yes," he said easily, flashing Gloria a brilliant smile. "The day I almost became a model." He shrugged out of his coat, hung it up on the hook attached to the booth, and eased himself in next to Nora. "How are you, Gloria?"

Gloria gave him a startled look. "Who, me? Oh, I'm fine."

"Tell me," he went on smoothly, "just exactly what does Nora Graham's assistant do?"

He continued to question her, drawing her out about her job, just as though he found it the most fascinating subject in the world. Gloria was literally glowing under all this unexpected attention, and it wasn't long before she was pouring out the story of her whole life.

Nora silently ground her back teeth together. This wasn't turning out at all the way she had anticipated. Here he was, charming the socks off Gloria, who was supposed to be *her* ally in the little charade she'd planned to embarrass him, and she was so rapt in the great man's charms that she totally ignored the dirty looks Nora was giving her until the waitress showed up to take Morgan's order, and Nora managed to catch her eye at last.

Gloria, unhappily, immediately misunderstood. She flushed guiltily, then bolted down the last few bites of her sandwich, and slid out of the booth.

"Well, it's been nice talking to you, Mr. Latimer," she muttered, backing hastily away. "I'd better get back to the office."

"Oh?" he said rising politely to his feet. "Must you?"

Nora was frantically trying to signal to her somehow that she didn't want to be left alone with him, but it wasn't working. With a sickly grin and a little wave, Gloria had already turned tail and was hurrying off.

When she was gone, Morgan settled himself easily in the seat across from Nora that Gloria had just vacated, propped his elbows on the table, laced his hands together under his chin, and gazed at her with a grave, rather quizzical expression. Avoiding his eye, Nora drank down the last of her coffee, and wiped her mouth with a napkin.

"Well," she said, edging her way toward the edge of the booth. "It's too bad you got here so late. As you can see, I've already finished my lunch, and it's time for me to get back."

A long arm shot out immediately, and she felt the grip of his hand on her wrist. "Don't go," he said in a low voice. "We haven't even had a chance to talk yet."

She pulled her arm away as though it had been burned. "Well, if you hadn't been so determined to charm my assistant, we might have," she retorted.

He smiled. "Well, if you hadn't brought her along, the problem wouldn't have arisen." He leaned back, suddenly serious. "Come on, Nora," he said softly. "Just listen to me for five minutes. Please."

Damn him, she thought, he seemed to know just how to get around her. What had happened to the clever plan she'd come up with, bringing Gloria along so they wouldn't be alone together? How had he worked it so that things were ending up exactly the way *he* wanted them? It was uncanny.

"Oh, all right," she said ungraciously.

She stayed in her seat, holding her spine rigid against the back of it, her hands folded on the table in front of her. The waitress came back then, with his order, and she, too, harried as she was with the luncheon rush, seemed to melt under the grin Morgan flashed at her. Nora watched with disgust as the girl simpered back at him, just as though he was exactly what she needed to brighten her whole day.

"The working girl's dream come true," Nora muttered under her breath, when the waitress was gone.

"What's that?" he said.

"Oh, nothing. Now, what was it you wanted to say to me?"

He eyed her carefully for a moment, refusing to be rushed, then said, "You're looking especially lovely today, Nora."

She stiffened a little more. Maybe he had Gloria and the waitress swooning for him, but she was armed against him by now, and well able to resist the practiced charm. Still, she was glad she'd worn the elegant new black suit, which fitted her so perfectly, and had somehow managed that morning to apply all that expensive makeup she'd bought in record time. Even the svelte new hairstyle had miraculously stayed in place.

In fact, she was becoming rather attached to her new, more sophisticated image. At least Morgan had done that for her. Although it was a lot of trouble, it was worth it. She'd made her mark in the world of advertising with the Latimer campaign, and it was time she looked the part. It certainly had nothing to do with *him* any longer.

Then what was she doing here? He'd finished half his steak sandwich by now, and still hadn't told her why he'd been so insistent on speaking to her. If he was that anxious, why was he stalling? Waiting for her to ask, most likely, and she clamped her jaw shut, determined not to give him the satisfaction. In fact, what she should do was just get up and walk out.

"The reason I called," he said, suddenly interrupting her thoughts, "was to explain to you about the *faux pas* I made last night." He shrugged. "It was stupid, I realize, but, believe me, I didn't mean it the way it sounded."

"Oh?" Nora raised one eyebrow. "Just what did you mean, then?" She put her hands flat on top of the table and leaned across it, her eyes narrowed. "When a man with as much power in the business as you have suggests to a mere flunky that he can help her with her career, I don't know what else it could mean."

"Don't you?" He swallowed the last of his lunch, and lit a cigarette, leaning back, perfectly relaxed. "It's true, isn't it? I *could* help you. And what would be wrong with it? I never said I'd want something from you in return." He cocked his head to one side, the silvery eyes crinkled with amusement. "That was all your idea."

Nora gripped the edge of the table, and raised her chin. "All right, then tell me this. Would you have made such an offer if I'd been a man?"

His eyes widened slightly at that, but he recovered quickly, making a diffident little gesture with one hand. "I might have."

Nora snorted. "I'll just bet."

"Well, at any rate, I sincerely apologize if I offended you." He flashed her the famous lopsided grin. "Which, apparently, I did. Now, can't we just forget it, and start all over again?"

Nora gazed at him dubiously, debating within herself. By now she wasn't sure what she thought, what she wanted. He *seemed* sincere, and in a way he was right. The idea that he wanted to make a trade, advancement in her career for sexual favors, had been her own interpretation. And even at the time, furious as she had been, she had thought it strange that a man like Morgan Latimer felt he had to buy his women.

Besides, there was no getting around the fact that she *was* attracted to him. Along with half the women in New York, she added wryly to herself. Still, what would be the harm? And he'd gone out of his way to clear up what he obviously thought of as a mere misunderstanding. How many of those adoring women would he have done that for?

"I like you, Nora," he was saying now. "I admire your professional ability, of course, but mainly I just want to get to know you better." He raised both hands in the air, palms facing her. "Honestly, that's all there is to it."

She was weakening, she knew it. Knowing full well it would be playing with fire to get involved with a man like this, but unable to stop herself, she relaxed the tense shoulder muscles, and jumped off the precipice.

"All right," she said with a sigh. "What did you have in mind?"

For the next few weeks Nora's life seemed to be full of Morgan Latimer. Hardly a day went by when she didn't at least talk to him on the telephone, and they saw each other almost every other night. She bought more new clothes—expensive, elegant suits and dresses—had her honey-colored hair styled so that she could manage it herself with only a weekly trip to the salon, and by now had learned to apply the makeup so deftly that it was second nature to her.

They went out to dinner at New York's finest restaurants, attended concerts, plays, musicals. They drove up to New England one Sunday afternoon to see the spectacular foliage, already turned from green to brilliant shades of red and gold in the crisp autumn weather. They found that they were both passionately fond of opera, and, of course, Morgan had box seats at the Met, the best in the house.

During those wonderful two weeks, she found him to be amusing, courteous, considerate, even affectionate. He always helped her in and out of cars, took her arm crossing the street, and when he helped her on or off with a coat his hands always lingered a little on her shoulders. But that was as far as it went. He seemed to consciously refrain from anything more intimate, as though trying to make good on his claim that he just wanted to get to know her better.

Although she appreciated this restraint in the beginning, after two weeks of it she was beginning to wonder if he intended that their relationship would always remain on that static plane; even if, perhaps, she didn't attract him physically. It also bothered her that although he always answered any direct question she put to him about his work, his present life, he never volunteered anything about his past, almost as though he were deliberately holding something back from her.

It was the middle of November now, a Friday. As usual, Morgan called her that morning at the office to ask her where she wanted to have dinner. On an impulse, she named the elegant French restaurant where they'd gone that first night.

He laughed. "You want to return to the scene of the crime?" he asked playfully.

"Not exactly. I just liked the way they did their steaks."

"All right. Whatever you say. I'll pick you up at your place around seven."

When they'd hung up, Nora sat there, her hand still on the receiver, staring into space, frowning a little. Just then, Jerry popped his head inside the door.

"Say, are we all set for the toy commercial today?" When she didn't even look up at him, he came ambling over to the desk, stood there staring down at her for a moment, then finally waved a hand in front of her face. "Hey, Nora. Anybody home?"

She jumped, and looked up at him. "Oh, sorry, Jerry. Guess I was daydreaming."

He perched on the edge of the desk. "I've noticed you doing a lot of that lately," he commented casually. When she didn't reply, he went on, "How's the great romance going?"

"What romance?" she said, in a wry tone. Then she could have bitten her tongue out for what the question implied. "Oh, you mean Morgan," she went on casually. "Fine, just fine."

"You don't sound fine. Come on, Nora, this is Uncle Jerry. What's wrong?"

Nora leaned back in her chair, and gave him a direct look. If she couldn't trust Jerry, who could she trust? She needed to talk about the situation with somebody.

"Jerry, do you think I'm attractive?"

"Sure," he said with a grin. "Your place or mine?"

"Oh, be serious. I mean, I know I'm not your type, one of your flamboyant redheads, but..." She shrugged. "You know what I mean."

Jerry eyed her carefully for a few moments. "I don't get it. Since you've finally decided to take a little trouble with yourself, for my money you've turned into a raving beauty." He leered at her suggestively, waggling his eyebrows. "In fact, maybe you *are* my type, after all."

"Oh, come on, Jerry. Be serious."

"I *am* serious! Hell, I figured by now you'd be beating the guy off."

"Well, to tell you the truth, I sort of did, too. But so far, I might as well be his sister for all the sparks I seem to raise in him."

"You like the guy? I mean, you're really interested in taking it on to another stage, romance wise?"

She nodded. "I guess so. I don't really know. You know, at first I was terrified of an involvement with him, afraid I was getting in over my head. Now, it seems if it's ever going to go anywhere, I'll have to make the first move."

"Well, why not?"

Her eyes flew open. "Come on, Jerry, don't be silly."

"Oh, I don't mean seduce him. Knowing you, I doubt if you want to take it quite *that* far, at least not just yet. But there are ways a woman can let a man know she's available for some kind of romancing. You know, the way you dress, the way you look at him, even a certain tone of voice. Maybe the poor guy's just waiting for a signal, after the way you treated him in the beginning." He slid off the desk. "Now, about that commercial..."

When they'd finished their business and Jerry had gone, she thought about what he'd said. Maybe it *was* her fault that Morgan was holding back. Come to think of it, she had been a little stiff with

GET A FREE TEDDY BEAR...

You'll love this plush, cuddly Teddy Bear, an adorable accessory for your dressing table, bookcase or desk. Measuring 5½" tall, he's soft and brown and has a bright red ribbon around his neck—he's completely captivating! And he's yours *absolutely free*, when you accept this no-risk offer!

AND FOUR FREE BOOKS!

Here's a chance to get **four free Harlequin Romance® novels** from the Harlequin Reader Service®—so you can see for yourself that we're like **no ordinary book club!**

We'll send you four free books...but you never have to buy anything or remain a member any longer than you choose. You could even accept the free books and cancel immediately. In that case, you'll owe nothing and be under **no obligation!**

Find out for yourself why thousands of readers enjoy receiving books by mail from the Harlequin Reader Service. They like the **convenience of home delivery...** they like getting the best new novels months before they're available in bookstores...and they love our **discount prices!**

Try us and see! Return this card promptly. We'll send your free books and a free Teddy Bear, under the terms explained on the back. We hope you'll want to remain with the reader service—but the choice is always yours! 116 CIH AJAV (U-H-R-05/93)

NAME

ADDRESS   APT

CITY   STATE   ZIP

Offer not valid to current Harlequin Romance® subscribers. All orders subject to approval.
© 1993 HARLEQUIN ENTERPRISES LIMITED   Printed in the U.S.A.

▼ CLAIM YOUR FREE BOOKS AND FREE GIFT! RETURN THIS CARD TODAY! ▼

NO OBLIGATION TO BUY!

him, even somewhat defensive, waiting for him to make a move, wondering how to handle it when it came.

Tonight, she vowed, it would be different. She'd wear the sexy bottle-green dress she'd bought for the Latimer party, and she'd try to dream up some of those signals Jerry mentioned.

That night they were seated at the same table they'd had before, right on the dance floor. Only this time, Nora had Martinis along with Morgan instead of wine, hoping to work up a kind of Dutch courage, and after dinner she actually drank the brandy she ordered.

"Shall we dance?" he said, when he'd finished his cigarette.

"Yes," she murmured. "I'd like that."

When he took her in his arms on the dimly lit dance floor, she suddenly knew instinctively that tonight no signals would be necessary. Either that, or she'd already sent enough so that he got the message. In any case, there was a subtle but quite definite difference in the way he held her tonight, and the minute she felt the tall, lean body pressing against hers, moving rhythmically to a slow dance tune, she realized how wrong she'd been to imagine he wasn't attracted to her.

As she melted against him, his hold on her tightened, he leaned his head down, and she felt the gentle rasp of his cheek against hers. She could hear his steady breathing in her ear, smell the clean scent of him, feel the warmth of his hand against her bare back.

They danced like that, their feet hardly moving at all, as though suspended in time, the electricity building between them, until finally, as though it had a will of its own, her hand went up to the back of his neck where the dark hair met the smooth skin, and she sensed the quick intake of his breath.

His lips were on her jaw now, moving toward her ear. "Shall we go?" he murmured in a low voice.

She pulled her head back and looked up at him, directly into the flecked gray eyes, alight now, even in the shadows, gleaming with an unmistakable desire. Her legs felt so weak that she wondered if they'd even carry her. She couldn't speak, could only nod wordlessly.

They retrieved her belongings at the table and went out through the dining room to the street. There was a cold nip in the November air, and she shivered a little, even in her heavy woolen coat. His arm came around her shoulders, pulling her tightly up against him as he hailed a passing taxi.

Nora stumbled into the backseat ahead of him, still in a daze. As they rode through the darkened streets towards her place, she couldn't think, didn't want to think. Here they were, on their way to she knew not what, his arm still around her, holding her close, her head resting on his shoulder. At this point she didn't believe she could manage to hold it up on her own.

Then she felt his hand on her face, forcing it around so that she was looking up at him. As their eyes met, her heart gave a great leap, and when his head came down and his lips were finally pressed against hers, gentle, soft, undemanding, she heard herself sigh with sheer contentment.

So this was what it was like to be kissed by a man like Morgan Latimer! There was no urgency in it, no uncontrollable thrusting, but the warmth that flooded through her told her all she needed to know, about his feelings as well as hers.

It was only a short ride, and when the cab pulled up in front of her building she stood on the pavement while Morgan paid the driver. Then he came over to her, put his hands on her shoulders, and looked down into her eyes, smiling the lop-sided smile she'd come to love so much. He didn't say a word, clearly leaving it up to her.

"Would you like to come in?" she said at last, in a husky voice.

He only nodded.

Slowly, they walked up the steps to the front door. She fumbled in her handbag for the key, but when she finally found it her hand was shaking so badly that she couldn't even get it inserted properly in the lock. He held out his hand for it, and, word-lessly, she gave it to him.

The minute they were inside her apartment, the door closed behind them, he turned to her. She'd left a night-light on, one dim lamp burning on her desk in a corner of the living room. In the shadows it cast, she could make out the question in his eyes. She hesitated for half a second, then with a sigh, closed her eyes and slumped toward him.

Even then, however, the small part of her mind that could still think clearly warned her that she could be making a very foolish mistake, that it wasn't too late to stop now, before it really got out of hand. Was she being too easy? Was this all part of his plan, to hold off until she was ripe for the picking?

Then his hands started traveling up and down her back, in slow, easy strokes. She could feel his mouth in her hair, on her cheeks, at her ear. Trembling, still uncertain, she buried her head in his shoulder. As though sensing her hesitation, the hands on her back stilled, and they just stood there quietly for a while.

Finally, unable to bear the suspense a moment longer, she raised her face to his. His face was in the shadows, the dim lamp casting just enough light on it to highlight the hollows under the prominent cheekbones, the firm jaw. He put his hands on either side of her face, gently, even lovingly, then slowly his face came closer, filling her whole field of vision.

When his mouth came down on hers at last, warm, tender, seeking, it seemed as though an explosion went off in her head. Her lips parted under his, and his tongue thrust past them into the interior of her mouth. She could feel the quick rise and fall of his chest, hear his rasping breath mingled with her own, and when one hand slid around to settle on her breast she knew she'd passed the point of no return.

"I want you, Nora," he murmured against her mouth. He raised his head and looked down at her, the gray eyes burning into hers. "I want you," he repeated huskily.

She searched those eyes, hoping to find... What? Affection? Tenderness? Love? At least some indication that he cared for her. But all she saw was the bright gleam of desire. It would have to be enough. He was clearly leaving it entirely up to her.

"Yes," she said at last. "Oh, yes, Morgan."

Slowly, he reached out and pulled the straps of the green dress down over her shoulders until it fell on the floor, and she stood before him dressed only in her lacy half slip and filmy bra. With his eyes fastened on her, he took off his jacket, loosened his tie, and started unbuttoning his shirt. Nora stared, entranced, as his bare broad chest was revealed.

After he had shrugged out of his shirt, he put his hands on her shoulders and ran them slowly downward until they came to rest on her breasts. Gasping with sheer pleasure, she closed her eyes and gave in completely to the delicious sensations aroused in her as his fingers brushed lightly over her hard nipples.

Then he crushed her to his bare chest, and his mouth descended on hers once again in a hot, open-mouthed kiss. His tongue darted inside her mouth, and the hands on her breasts kneaded and stroked until she thought she would go mad with the fire that was coursing through her bloodstream.

They sank slowly to the floor. He knelt before her and unfastened the bra, then clasped her so closely in his arms that her naked breasts were crushed against his chest. Slowly, he eased her down on her back and leaned over her, bracing himself with one hand flat on the floor, while the other explored her body eagerly, her breasts, her stomach, her thighs.

"Touch me, Nora," he whispered.

She smiled, and reached up to run her hands through his dark crisp hair until it fell over his forehead. Then she placed her palms on his broad chest, moved them over his tautly muscled arms and shoulders and back. His skin was smooth and hot and slightly damp, and quivered under her light touch. When she reached the waistband of his pants, she gave him a shy, inquiring look. He nodded his encouragement.

She unbuckled his belt, then, and slipped her fingers inside the loosened waistband to feel the rough hair that began there on his lower abdomen. With a sharp indrawn gasp, he put his hand over hers and pressed it tight against his body, forcing it lower, until she became fully aware of his intense need of her.

With a groan, he moved away, and slid out of his pants and jockey shorts. When he came back to her, he kissed her on the mouth, then lowered his lips to her throat, her breast, and with one hand firmly clasping the full firm mound from underneath, he opened his mouth to cover the throbbing peak, suckling there until Nora began to twist beneath him, hardly able to endure the sharp stabs of desire that coursed through her. He moved his lips to her other breast, and slid his hand down over her rib cage, her hips, the inside of her thighs, until it finally came to rest between them.

She cried out at the sheer unexpected thrill of ecstasy his touch aroused in her, and at last he covered her body with his own, and she felt his hard pulsing desire throb against her.

"Oh, please, Morgan," she begged. "Please. Now."

Slowly, he entered her, and as the passionate crescendo began to build with each thrust Nora went limp and weak with the sensations that filled her entire being, mind, body and soul, until finally she reached the pinnacle of excruciating tension. She couldn't stop herself from crying out her joy at that glorious climax. She felt herself shattering into a million pieces, heard Morgan's answering shout of release, and then sank down into near oblivion, satisfied at last.

She lay still, panting in his arms, for several long minutes, while he stroked her hair and face tenderly, speaking her name in a low, intimate voice. He eased himself off her, and they lay together, closely entwined, until she grew drowsy, felt herself drifting off into a deep, dreamless sleep.

Some time during the night she woke up to the most marvelous sensations, a warm body at her side, long rough legs entangled with her own, a large hand resting on her bare breast.

Morgan! Her eyes flew open, and she raised her head slightly to glance over at the man sleeping peacefully by her side. The dim lamp was still burning, the outlines of his naked body clearly visible. What a beautiful man he was! The broad bony shoulders, the strong chest muscles, the flat abdomen. She longed to reach out and touch him, to run her hands up and down that strong hard frame, so different from her own.

Suddenly the hand on her breast tightened possessively, and an arm slid beneath her neck. When she looked over at him, one eye was open, and there was no mistaking what she saw there.

"Come here," he murmured sleepily, reaching out for her.

"Morgan, it's freezing in here."

He sat up. "Then let's go to bed."

They walked hand in hand, naked, down the hall to her bedroom, and the minute they were under the covers, she was in his arms again. His hands and mouth began to explore her body as though he were trying to memorize it, and this time their love-making was slower, not quite so urgent as before—and even more satisfying.

CHAPTER SIX

THE next morning when Nora awoke to the cold light of day, he was gone, and even though the memory of what had happened last night lingered on, still vivid in her mind, she could hardly believe she'd actually gone through with it.

She buried her head in her pillow, and groaned. What had she done? How could she have been so foolish, so *easy*? It was so unlike her. What had happened to cautious, cool, sensible Nora Graham? It had to be the Martinis before dinner, the wine during, the brandy afterward, the new clothes, like an unfamiliar second skin.

She sat up in bed, clutching the covers to her naked body. Sure, she'd wanted a little romance, but to sleep with him the first time he kissed her? And on the living-room floor, to boot! Of course, that was only the first time. She groaned again.

But was she really sorry? As she fought past the sickening sense of guilt and shame at her own reckless behaviour, she glanced over at the pillow where he had lain, the indentation of his dark head still visible, and memory came flooding back. It had been, without a doubt, the most heavenly experience of her life, one that she wouldn't have traded for anything in the world. Her first real experience with lovemaking, and what lovemaking it had been!

What bothered her, however—even made her feel a little cheap—was that she'd been such a push-over, just like all the rest, a one-night stand that would probably never be repeated. She'd been dazzled by his charm and seductive appeal, but the decision had been a conscious one. And even if she never heard from him again she had a lovely memory to treasure for the rest of her life.

Of course she'd probably signed the death sentence to any hope of a serious relationship with Morgan. That had been part of the bargain. And if you didn't expect anything, you couldn't be disappointed. She glanced at the bedside clock. It was past ten, but thank heavens it was Saturday. She could sleep all day if she wanted to. She lay back down in the warm bed, and snuggled under the covers.

She had just drifted off into that half sleep where reality blurred into dreamland, when the telephone jangled beside her bed. She opened one eye, debating whether to answer it. But it could be her mother calling about her father. If he'd had another attack...

She sat bolt upright, and grabbed the receiver. "Hello," she said apprehensively.

"Good morning. Did I wake you up?"

Her heart gave a great leap. "Morgan," she said. "No. I'm awake." She laughed. "Although I'm not actually out of bed yet."

"Mm," he said. "Sounds enticing."

Nora lay her head back on the pillows, grinning foolishly, filled with a wild sense of elation. He *had* called!

"How are you this morning?" he asked cheerily.

"I—I'm fine."

"You don't sound too sure."

There was a hint of amusement in his voice, and Nora bridled. She could picture him in her mind, tall and self-assured, a little half smile on his face. Was he condescending to her because she'd been so easy?

"Well, I am sure," she retorted. "Quite sure."

He hesitated a moment, then went on in a lower, more intimate voice. "About last night. No regrets?"

"No," she said. She had nothing to be ashamed of. No one had been hurt, and it had been wonderful. She was a grown woman, after all, not a blushing adolescent. And as far as she could tell, there wasn't much blushing going on among adolescent girls these days, anyway. "None at all," she repeated firmly.

"Good," he said with satisfaction. "I hope it was only the first of many more."

"Yes," she said, melting again. She felt as though she was floating on a warm, soft cloud.

"How do you feel about sailing?" he was asking her now.

"I don't know. I've never tried it."

"The family own a good-sized sailing boat that we keep moored on the north shore of Long Island. It's a perfect day for it; sunny, but a good wind. Interested?"

"Well, I'm game to try, just so long as you're not relying on me to be much help. I can follow orders pretty well, though."

"That's good enough for me. I'll pick you up in an hour. Wear something warm."

* * *

That evening they had dinner at the seafood restaurant attached to the marina where Morgan kept his boat. Sitting across from him now, with the lights of the small harbor winking down below, worn out from the sheer hard labor involved in sailing a thirty-foot ketch in a brisk breeze, Nora felt as though she'd died and gone to heaven.

They had just finished a delicious meal of freshly caught Maine lobster. Morgan seemed relaxed and content, puffing on his usual after-dinner cigarette, his dark hair still tousled from the breeze. He was wearing blue denim jeans and a heavy white turtle-neck sweater, and Nora was trying to make up her mind whether he looked more devastating in casual clothes than he did in more formal wear, finally deciding it was a toss-up.

"Are you worn out?" he asked her now, catching her eye.

"A little. But it's a good kind of tired."

"I worked you pretty hard today."

She smiled. "Yes, you did. In fact, I've been wondering if you treat your employees the same way. You know, 'Tote that barge, lift that bale.'"

He grinned back at her. "Oh, I run a tight ship at the office, too. It's the only way to get the job done."

"I only hope I wasn't more hindrance than help. I didn't realize how complicated sailing was."

He reached across the table and put his hand over hers. "You did fine," he said softly. "You're a good sport, and that's what really counts."

Their eyes met, and Nora could feel herself starting to melt under that silvery gaze. "I'm glad," she murmured.

His fingers were making circles on the back of her hand. "Are you ready to go?" he asked.

She could only nod, hardly trusting herself to speak at all at this point. Morgan signaled to the waitress for the bill, and while he paid it Nora excused herself for a trip to the powder room. Washing her hands, she glanced in the mirror to adjust the scarf she'd tied around her head, and noticed how flushed her face looked, how bright the green eyes were.

I'm in love with him, she mouthed silently at her reflection. Immediately, a small stab of anxiety tore at her heart. But where were they going? Where would it end? What could possibly be in it for her but heartbreak? She shook her head, and turned away. She wouldn't think about that. All she knew was that she was happier than she'd ever been in her life, and nothing on earth could make her give it up.

He was waiting for her near the front entrance, and they went out into the parking lot, where they'd left the gray Mercedes. Although it was only seven o'clock, it was quite dark by now, the November dusk falling early. They walked slowly toward the car, their hands clasped together, and when they reached it Morgan stopped short and turned to her.

He reached out to slide the silk scarf on her head down around her neck, then ran his fingers through her thick honey-colored mass. "I love your hair," he said. "It feels just like fine silk." His arms came around her waist, pulling her lower body up against his, and he gazed down into her eyes. "Last night was wonderful," he murmured.

"Yes," she whispered.

She searched his face, barely visible in the pale glow of the lights coming from the restaurant. Every feature had become intimately familiar to her by now—the high-bridged nose, the sharp cheekbones with the hollows underneath, the firm jaw and chin, the beautiful eyes. Maybe it was possible that he loved her, or could learn to love her, and maybe not. But whatever happened, she knew she was right to take that chance.

He leaned over to kiss her lightly on the mouth, and reached one hand underneath her heavy sweater to run it lightly over her bare midriff, just brushing the underside of her breasts. Nora's head was swimming, her heart pounding, her blood on fire.

At that moment the headlights of another car appeared, coming straight toward them. Quickly, Morgan withdrew his hands.

"We'd better get out of here," he said, with a laugh. "Before we get ourselves arrested."

For the next several weeks, Nora felt as though she were living in some kind of dreamworld. They continued to see each other almost every other day, and by now Morgan had become so much a part of her life that she wondered how she'd ever tolerated the old existence without him.

By tacit consent, each evening they were together, Morgan would come home with her, and although he never stayed the entire night she soon became used to having him in her bed. She'd never lived on such intimate terms with a man before, and it was a heady experience for her that was only slightly marred by her occasional nagging doubts about where it all was heading, or how he really felt about her.

One night they were having dinner at what she'd come to think of as "their" French restaurant, when a tall, very beautiful brunette came walking over to their table in the middle of the meal. The moment Morgan caught sight of her, the gray eyes glazed over, and his jaw became set in a familiar way.

"Morgan, darling!" she cried, when she reached their table. She leaned down, threw her arms around his neck, and kissed him soundly on the mouth.

Obviously annoyed, he jerked his head back, then grabbed her hands away, and rose quickly to his feet. Nora just sat there watching, wondering what he was going to do. From the angry look in his eyes and the firm set of his jaw, she was afraid of a scene, but in the very next moment he was giving the brunette a thin smile.

"Hello, Margot," he said. The smile was forced, and there was a hard edge in his voice, but the mask had slid firmly in place again. He turned to Nora. "Nora, this is Margot Farragut."

And that was all. Nora sat there listening while they chatted for a few minutes about mutual acquaintances, and when Margot left to join her party Morgan offered no explanation of her status in his life except a brief murmur about an old friend, and at that point Nora began to see red.

"What does that mean?" she asked.

He shrugged. "Just what I said. Margot is an old friend of mine."

"How close a friend?"

His face closed down, not quite a frown, but obviously annoyed at the question. He didn't say anything for several moments. Slowly and carefully he reached into his jacket pocket for his cigarettes, lit one, shook out the match and dropped it in the ashtray. Then, suddenly, he smiled. He reached across the table to take her hand.

"You're not jealous, are you?" he asked in a teasing voice.

"No. Of course not," was the prompt reply. "But if a gorgeous man came running over here and began pawing me, I think you might be mildly curious about our relationship."

He started to laugh, but sobered instantly when he saw the look on her face. "Of course I would," he admitted. "You're right." He lifted his broad shoulders. "What can I say? A long time ago—years by now—Margot and I had a little fling. It never amounted to anything serious, and we parted on good terms. No animosity on either side, and no regrets."

Nora thought this over. He seemed sincere. Actually, he'd been quite annoyed by the way the brunette had burst in on them, and Nora was certain there was no love lost there, no reason for suspicion or jealousy. Still, something about his attitude bothered her.

"Tell me, Morgan," she said slowly. "Have all your relationships been so trivial?"

His gray eyes narrowed at her. "What do you mean by trivial?"

"Well, hasn't there ever been a woman you felt you couldn't live without?"

"No!" he snapped. He ground out his cigarette in long, slow jabs. "That's not in the cards for me."

Nora's heart sank. "I see," she said in a small voice. "Do you mind telling me why?"

He braced his elbows on the table and gave her a long look, his forehead wrinkled. "Listen, Nora," he said at last. "I've tried to be honest with you right from the start. I'm very attracted to you. You know that. I love being with you. I want us to keep on seeing each other, but..." His voice trailed off.

"That sounds suspiciously like an ultimatum," she said softly. "Or a threat."

His eyes flew open. "No," he stated in a positive tone. "You're wrong. I'd never do that. I just wanted to make my position quite clear so there'd be no misunderstanding."

"By your position," she said in a dry tone, "I assume you mean your terms."

"Nora, don't," he said with a sigh. "Don't spoil things. Can't we just enjoy what we have?"

She looked at him. From the concerned expression on his face she knew he was telling the truth, that he did care about her. But he meant what he said, and her blood ran cold at the thought of losing him. She couldn't do that. Not now. She was in too deep, the commitment already made. It would have to be his terms or nothing. At least for now.

She forced out a smile. "All right," she said. "I get the picture. Don't worry about it."

Still, he looked troubled. "Damn it, Nora, I don't mean to sound dictatorial. I'm very happy with the way things are between us, but I want you to be happy, too."

"It's all right," she said. Then she smiled sweetly, and added, "For now."

He gave her a startled look, then threw his head back and laughed. "That's what I love about you. You always manage to surprise me."

The tense moment passed, and it was only later that she realized what it was that really troubled her about the scene with Margot. It wasn't jealousy at all, but the way he had been able to cover up his annoyance at Margot's appearance, so quickly, so instinctively.

She remembered, too, how he'd dealt with the gossip columnist the first time he'd taken her to that very same restaurant. Once again, his irritation had been patent, but he'd covered it up immediately, and even managed to be pleasant to the little worm. Was this iron control an admirable trait? Who *was* the real Morgan Latimer?

As time went by, these small evasions began to bother her more and more. She was head over heels in love with him, had even begun to believe there was a possibility their affair might lead to a permanent commitment, perhaps even marriage. Neither his ardor in their lovemaking nor his apparent pleasure in being with her had dimmed even slightly. But in order to take it the one step further she longed for, she felt that somehow she had to penetrate those defenses he'd erected around his inner self, and find out what was beneath the mask.

Finally, the opportunity presented itself. It was the middle of December, almost Christmas, and one Sunday night she'd cooked dinner for him in her apartment. They'd just finished the simple meal of steak, baked potato and green salad, and were sitting across from each other at the table by the window in the living room, looking out over the lights of the city.

"Do you have any plans for Christmas?" he asked.

"Well, I usually spend a few days with my family up in Vermont, although nothing definite has been settled."

"Would you consider putting off your visit and spending Christmas Eve at my place? It'll just be the family—my brother, Owen, Anne, and her husband and kids."

"Yes," Nora agreed quickly. "I'd like that very much." Then, sensing a perfect opening, she plunged ahead. "Were the three of you very close when you were children?"

He waved a dismissive hand in the air. "Oh, we had our share of bickering." He chuckled. "Even one or two knock-down, drag-out fights with Owen. But he's an artist, not a fighter, so they didn't amount to much."

Nora propped her elbow on the table, put her chin in her hand, and gave him an encouraging smile. "And you are? A fighter, I mean. I wonder why?"

He shrugged. "Who knows?"

His smile remained in place, but she knew him well enough by now to realize that the mask had settled once again. She could see it in the very slight narrowing of the gray eyes, which took on a rather hard, glazed, almost warning look, and the slightly more determined set to his jaw.

But this time she was determined not to give up so easily. She had surmised that his mother had died when he was quite young, since on the few occasions he did mention his childhood he never spoke of her. Actually, the references to his father were so scanty as to be practically nonexistent, but at least he seemed to have been present while the children were growing up.

"Would you say that's a trait you inherited from your father?" she asked carefully.

"I hope not," he said in a clipped voice. He got up from his chair. "How about some more coffee? We have plenty of time." He walked over to the sideboard, poured himself out another cup from the carafe, then came back to stand beside the table, looking down at her. "Have you decided which movie you want to see?"

Nora stared up at him. He'd done it again! Irritation rose up in her, making her reckless. She leaned back in her chair, folded her arms across her chest, and forced him to meet her eyes.

"Morgan, why do you always avoid answering me when I ask you a direct question about your past?"

He gave her the famous lopsided grin. "Do I do that?"

But she was not to be sidetracked this time. "Yes, you do," she replied tartly. She reached out to take his hand. "Morgan, I..." She couldn't quite say it, couldn't tell him she loved him. "Surely you know how much I care about you," she began again. "I'm not quizzing you out of idle curiosity. I just want to know you better."

He gazed down at her, his eyes hard. "You know everything you need to know about me. I'm thirty-seven years old, and I'm sure you're aware I haven't lived like a monk all these years, but I have nothing to be ashamed of. No wife and children lurking in the background, no secret love nest tucked away. I've never been in jail, or even arrested. I'm not hiding anything from you that could remotely have a bearing on our relationship. I just don't want to discuss it. I *won't* discuss it. And if that's not good enough for you, then . . ." His voice trailed off.

He went to his chair, and they sat there in stony silence for a good two minutes. Morgan smoked and sipped at his coffee, while Nora stared down at her empty plate. Her first reaction was a terrible fear. If that's not good enough—then what? Was he threatening her? Back off or I walk out of your life? She didn't think she could bear that.

Finally, he drained his coffee, stubbed out his cigarette, and got up to come around behind her. He leaned down, crossing his arms in front of her and put his face against hers. One hand brushed her hair back, and she felt his warm breath in her ear.

"You know I'm crazy about you, Nora," he said, in a low voice. "We've got a marvelous thing going for us just the way it is. Don't spoil it by digging into things that don't matter."

She twisted her head around so that their lips met. His mouth grazed hers lightly, and the hand on her cheek moved down to grasp the base of her neck. As the kiss deepened, his hand slid inside the low opening of her silk shirt, under the lacy bra, and when she felt his long fingers making slow lazy circles on her bare breast she knew she was lost, that she'd give him anything, do anything he asked, just to keep him with her like this.

"Shall we bag the movie?" he said in her ear.

The next day Nora called her parents to let them know she wouldn't be coming up to Vermont until Christmas Day. She had been so thrilled at Morgan's unexpected invitation to spend Christmas Eve with him and his family that she hadn't even thought at the time how it might affect her parents.

"I hope you're not too disappointed," she said to her mother.

"Of course not, darling. The Parkers have invited us to a small party anyway, and then we'll go on to the midnight church service as usual. I'm just pleased that you've met someone you're interested in." She laughed. "In fact, since I've been the one promoting it for such a long time I can hardly complain."

"Well, so long as you're sure. Do you think Dad will mind?"

"Oh, I can handle your father. I'll tell you what, though, if you're worried about him, it would please him enormously if you could talk your young man into coming up here with you on Christmas Day."

"I'll try," Nora replied. "And I'll be thinking of you both on Christmas Eve, anyway."

She was pleased at her mother's invitation. Actually, she had already thought of asking Morgan to go home with her for Christmas dinner, and now, with her mother's encouragement, she decided she just might do it. All he could do was say no, and so far he'd been so agreeable to all her requests that she didn't think she'd have to twist his arm.

All her requests but one. The memory of the rather unpleasant conversation they'd had last night still gnawed at the back of her mind. Clearly, the "No Trespassing" signs were erected so firmly that she'd never get past them, and unless she wanted more awkward scenes like that one she'd have to back off.

He'd said he wasn't married, nor involved with anyone else. His past didn't sound in the least lurid. But something in it obviously still had the power to affect him deeply, and she couldn't help wondering what wound could have been so hurtful that it had erected such a powerful barrier between him and his emotions.

Morgan had warned her that his family always made Christmas Eve a rather formal affair, so she had bought a new dress for the occasion, a lovely shade of deep gold velvet with a low scoop neck outlined in sequins, and tiny cap sleeves. A fitted bodice tapered down to her narrow waist, below which the full skirt fell gracefully down to mid-calf. She didn't own any good jewelry, but the dress was so perfect that it didn't really need anything more.

She had winced at the price, almost a full month's salary, but the look in Morgan's eyes when he came to pick her up that evening made it more than worthwhile.

Morgan, as always, looked devastating in his dark formal suit, perfectly tailored, with an immaculate white shirt that gleamed against his tanned face. The cuffs were fastened with heavy solid-gold cufflinks set with onyx, which, except for the thin gold watch on his wrist, was all the jewelry he wore.

He had picked her up at seven, a full hour earlier than the others, who weren't due to arrive until eight o'clock. It would be her first visit to his Park Avenue apartment, which she'd been dying to see for ages, and was thrilled at the chance to explore it on her own.

"I wanted to give you a tour of the place before the family get here," he explained, on the way up in the elevator. "It'll be sheer pandemonium once those kids of Anne's get a look at all the packages under the tree."

It was everything she could possibly have imagined it would be, on the top floor, overlooking Central Park, the lights of the city glowing through the wide bank of windows at one end of the long living room. A grand piano stood in one corner, an enormous tree in the corner opposite, already brightly decorated, with blinking white and gold lights, and an enormous star at the very top, which almost reached to the high ceiling.

The room was decorated predominantly in cool tones of grays and blues, with an occasional bright spot of color in the cushions scattered on the wide, low couches flanking the stone fireplace, and the paintings on the walls.

"Well," Morgan said, after she'd had several minutes to wander around exploring. "What do you think?"

She turned to him. "I think it's wonderful. It looks just like you, Morgan."

He laughed. "What does that mean?"

She cocked her head to one side and gave him a teasing look. "Oh, you know, rather hidden, secretive, not revealing much on the surface." His smile began to fade, and laughing, she slid her arms around his waist. "But with definite flashes of fire underneath," she added.

"That's better," he said, giving her a quick peck on the forehead. "Now, how about the rest of the place?"

She nodded happily, and they walked slowly up the two broad steps to the raised dining room, the long table already gaily decorated with holly, poinsettias, and with plates of cold canapés set out on top of a snowy white damask tablecloth.

"My," she said, impressed. "Did you do all this yourself?"

"Hardly," he said, in an amused tone. "Anne and my housekeeper have been working like beavers every day for the past week on the decorating and the food. I can't take credit for any of it."

By the time they'd finished the tour, the comfortable library where he worked at home, his own large, immaculate bedroom and guest room, both with their own baths, it was almost eight o'clock.

"We'll save the champagne until later," he said, leading the way back to the kitchen. "But we can have one glass of wine on our own before the others get here. They're usually late, so we have plenty of time."

The kitchen was a marvel of the most modern, up-to-date equipment, spotlessly kept. Morgan went to the fridge, took out a bottle of white wine, and filled two of the glasses standing on the marble-topped counter. He handed one to her, then held his own up in a toast.

"To us," he said softly.

"Yes," she replied, as the glasses clinked together. "To us."

After one sip, Morgan set his glass down on the counter. "Stay right there," he said. "I have something for you."

Nora watched him go with a clutch of apprehension, and hastily took a healthy swallow of her wine. She was certain he'd gone to get her Christmas present, and she had come empty-handed. After racking her brains for weeks trying to think of an appropriate gift for him, she'd finally decided not to get him anything. What could she buy a man who already had everything?

Then, a week ago, she'd come up with the bright idea of knitting him a scarf. She'd bought the finest cashmere yarn and tiny needles, going half blind every evening she wasn't either out with him or working, and still it was only half done. She'd debated wrapping it up and giving it to him anyway, in its half-finished condition, but decided in the end that that was too gauche, even for her.

He came back carrying a flat oblong package, and silently handed it to her. She gave him a worried look, and started to explain to him about the scarf, but he put a finger on her lips after the first few words, silencing her.

"Never mind about that," he said. "You can tell me later."

She looked down at the package in her hands. "Shall I open it now, then?"

He nodded. Carefully, she untied the glossy silver bow and peeled off the red paper to reveal a white box, the name of Manhattan's most exclusive jeweler engraved on the cover in gold script lettering. With her heart in her mouth, she lifted the lid, and slowly pushed aside the layer of tissue paper.

When she saw what was inside she could only gasp and stare. There on a bed of satin was a diamond pendant hung on a thin gold chain. One large diamond was set in the center, encircled by a row of smaller gems.

"Morgan," she faltered, gazing up at him. "I don't know what to say."

"Say you like it. Do you? If not, we can always exchange it."

She lifted the delicate chain out of the box, and held it in her hand. "I *love* it!" she exclaimed. "Who wouldn't? But it's far too much. I don't feel right accepting such an expensive gift from you."

"Don't be silly," he said with finality. He took the pendant from her. "Turn around and let me fasten it for you."

She turned away from him, her head still in a whirl, bent her head, and raised her arms to lift the heavy fall of hair away from the back of her neck while Morgan slid the chain around it. When he had finished, she looked down to see the diamond circle sparkling there, just above the low bodice of her dress.

His hands moved to her shoulders, and she felt his lips pressing on the crook of her neck. There was something symbolic about that small act, as though fastening the chain around her neck somehow tied her irrevocably to him. With a sigh, she leaned back against him, and when his arms came around her, his hands settling over her breasts, a familiar warmth stirred within her.

"Now——" Morgan breathed in her ear "—you belong to me."

Just then the doorbell rang, breaking the spell. With a nervous laugh, Nora turned around to face him. He was gazing down at her with a look in his eyes that she'd never seen before, a look full of such yearning that it had to be love. She put a hand on the side of his face and kissed him.

"Thank you, Morgan," she said. "It's beautiful. I love it." The chimes rang out again. "Now, hadn't we better answer the door?"

Morgan hadn't been exaggerating when he'd described the advent of his niece and three young nephews as pandemonium. They ranged in age from five to twelve, old enough to appreciate the ritual ceremony of gift giving, but not yet jaded by teenage sophistication.

The plan was to let the children open their gifts first, then eat the late supper Anne and Morgan's housekeeper had prepared. Morgan had already uncorked the champagne, cooling in the ice bucket on the dining-room sideboard, and poured them each a glass.

After the Christmas toast, Owen, the artist of the family, went to the piano and began to play carols softly in the background, while Morgan organized the children's gifts. Nora sat down on the couch beside Anne, who was explaining that her husband was still out on the street looking for a parking spot.

"I kept telling him we should take a taxi," she said, with an exaggerated sigh. "But would he listen to me? He's as bad as Morgan when it comes to stubbornness."

Morgan whirled around. "Who, me?" he demanded, hurt.

"Bobby!" Anne cried, looking past him. "Put that package down this minute! It's not your turn." She frowned at Morgan. "If you're going to supervise those kids, you'd better pay more attention to what they're doing."

Nora watched the byplay in a euphoric state of serene happiness. As an only child, she'd missed out on the give and take of family life, and now, with the piano tinkling in the background, the excited children crouched in front of the tree, Morgan and his sister bickering, she felt they were including her as a full member.

Meanwhile, the doorbell chimes rang out. "That'll be Mark," Anne said, rising to her feet, and heading for the foyer. "He probably had to park clear across town, and ended up taking a taxi here, anyway."

Owen got up from the piano, and came to stand before Nora. "That's a lovely pendant you're wearing, Nora," he said. "It just suits your..."

At that moment, he raised his eyes and gazed past her, a look of sheer horror slowly spreading across his mild features. Alarmed, Nora turned around quickly to see Anne walking back inside the living room. She was followed by a tall man who was definitely not her husband, Mark.

There was a sudden deathly stillness in the room. Even the children were quiet, as though they sensed danger of some kind. Nora stared at the man, wondering who he could be that the others were so stunned at his appearance.

In the hushed silence she heard a sudden loud cracking sound. She looked over at Morgan, still standing motionless by the tree. He was ashen, his face drawn and haggard, every muscle tense, his eyes two gray slits of fury. He was still holding the broken champagne glass in his upraised hand, a bright red trail of blood already seeping down his wrist.

He began slowly walking toward Anne, who quickly stepped out of the way, until he was directly confronting the strange man, separated from him by only a few feet. He was almost as tall as Morgan, much older, but with a strong resemblance to him.

For several heart-stopping seconds the two men simply stood there, staring at each other. Morgan's back was toward Nora now, so that she couldn't see his face, but from the tense, stiff way he held himself, just like a wild animal at bay, defending his territory, his hands clenched into fists at his sides, she knew he was terribly upset. The other man was smiling weakly.

Finally, Morgan took one more step toward him. "What the hell are you doing here?" he ground out, in a low, menacing voice.

CHAPTER SEVEN

THE smile gradually faded from the older man's face. For several long seconds, he and Morgan stood there staring at each other, like two marble statues, neither making a move toward the other.

Nora, stunned by this sudden turn of events, could only watch the striking tableau spread out before her. A part of her mind was oddly detached, as though she were in the audience watching a drama being played out on a stage. After all, she was the outsider here, definitely a non-participant.

But another part of her was struck more than anything else by the startling resemblance between the two men, and her immediate conclusion was that it had to be Morgan's father. Although his dark hair was streaked with gray, his face lined, his carriage more stooped, and he had an air of defeat about him that she couldn't possibly associate with Morgan, the facial features and general build were almost identical.

Then she noticed the blood, still flowing a bright red from the cut on Morgan's hand, and starting to drip on the gray carpet. She should do something about it, but she was held immobile in the fraught silence, as though by an invisible thread.

Finally, the older man raised a hand, and forced out another pitiful smile. "Well, now, Morgan," he said in a halting voice. "I am your father, after all."

Ignoring him completely, Morgan turned on Anne. "Is this your doing?" he ground out in a low voice.

Anne shook herself, as though awakening from a bad dream. "Oh, of course not," she said irritably. "Do you think I'd invite him here without telling you first, knowing how you felt about him?"

Morgan turned to glare at his brother. "Owen?"

Owen's mild blue eyes were still registering astonishment, and he raised his hands in the air, defensively. "No, sir. Not me, Morgan. I know better than that." He walked slowly to Morgan's side. "Come on, you'd better let me take care of that cut."

He took Morgan by the arm, but when it became obvious that his brother had no intention of moving Owen shrugged, took out a white handkerchief from his pant pocket, and wrapped it around the bleeding hand.

Anne had gone to her father's side. "Well, Dad," she said, her voice high and wavering with false heartiness. "Now that you're here, why don't you come and sit down?"

"No!" Morgan shouted angrily.

Anne turned on him. "Morgan, don't be like that. He's your father—*our* father—whatever you might feel about him."

They stood there facing each other, their eyes locked together, neither giving an inch, both of them Latimers to the core. At that moment one of the children began to cry. Morgan swiveled his head around in the direction of the tree. He hesitated a second, a look of painful indecision on his face. His shoulders sagged, and he made a helpless gesture of defeat. Then, suddenly, he whirled around, and stalked out of the room.

Nora stared after him. In a moment, she heard the front door slam. Still paralyzed with shock, she couldn't move for what seemed like an eternity. She gazed around the room, which now seemed full of strangers. With Morgan's departure all the life and warmth had gone out of it for her, and she finally stirred into action.

"I'm sorry," she muttered, making a dash for the chair where she'd left her coat. "I've got to go after him."

Without waiting for their reaction to her announcement, she grabbed her coat, shrugged into it on her way to the front hall, and went out into the corridor, closing the door quietly behind her.

There was no sign of Morgan. She jabbed the elevator button and stood there waiting, tapping her foot impatiently on the tiled floor, buttoning her heavy coat. Finally, the elevator came. She stepped inside and was immediately borne downward.

In the main lobby, she hurried to the entrance of the building. It was snowing lightly outside, and she had neither a scarf to put over her head, nor an umbrella. She pushed open the heavy glass door, and went out under the protective canopy. She saw the uniformed doorman standing at the curb, and ran over to him.

"Did you see Mr. Latimer come out?" she asked breathlessly.

"Yes, ma'am," he replied. He pointed at the traffic-clogged street. "There he is now, just getting into that taxi."

She spotted him, then, halfway inside the back seat of a taxi double-parked in front, and made straight for it. "Morgan!" she called, waving. "Wait for me!"

His head turned, and for a moment he hesitated. He was bending over, one foot already inside the cab, and Nora prayed he wouldn't keep going and leave before she reached him. Slowly, he straightened up and stood there facing her until she reached his side.

"Morgan," she said, panting. She peered up into his face. "Where are you going?"

His lips curled in a humorless smile. "I'm going to get drunk," he stated flatly.

"Let me come with you."

From the starkly cold look on his face, she knew he was going to say "no." Searching her mind for some way to persuade him, desperate not to let him go without her, she finally gave up and acted from pure instinct.

She raised her hands and placed them on either side of his face, gazing directly into the wintry gray eyes. "Please, Morgan," she said. "I want to help you."

"I don't need your help," he said coldly. "There's nothing you can do. This is something I've got to work out on my own."

Just then there was a sudden honking of horns, and the taxi driver leaned his head out of the window. "Hey, buddy," he called. "Will you please make up your mind? I gotta get outa here."

Still Morgan hesitated, and Nora knew she was right to persist. If he really hadn't wanted her with him, he would have been long gone.

"Please," she begged. "I want to be with you. I—I love you, Morgan."

"All right," he said at last. "Suit yourself."

With a curt nod, he stepped aside, and she scrambled into the backseat. He got in beside her, slamming the door shut, and she settled back, with a sigh of relief. The minute the door was closed, the driver shot off like a rocket.

"Where to?" he called over his shoulder.

Morgan gave him the name of a well-known cocktail lounge in a seedy part of town. Apparently, he was in no mood to be seen at the more elegant places he was used to patronizing.

They rode along in silence, not touching, not speaking a word. After a few blocks, Nora glanced over at him. His head was pressed against the window, and he was staring out morosely at the falling snow, his chin in his hand, lost in his own terrible thoughts.

But at least he'd let her come. She'd have to be satisfied with that.

They sat at a back table in the crowded bar, away from the noise. Nora ordered a glass of white wine, Morgan a double bourbon, neat. When it came, he downed it in one long swallow, then raised his hand for a refill.

"Just keep them coming," he told the waitress, when she arrived with a fresh drink.

Nora sat helplessly across from him, trying not to stare, but watching him out of the corner of her eye while she sipped on the wine she didn't want and wondering if he was ever even going to speak to her again.

"Morgan, please tell me what's troubling you," she said finally. "Let me help you."

He raised his glass and drained his drink. "I told you once, Nora, that I didn't want to discuss my past. Tonight you got a look at one good reason why. I'm sorry you had to witness it, but the damage is done now." He lit a cigarette, and gazed at her through the curls of smoke. "Just remember that I didn't ask you to come with me. You were the one who insisted on tagging along."

In desperation, she decided to try a different tack. "How's your hand?"

He held it up and stared at it as though he'd forgotten all about it. Slowly, he unwrapped the blood-soaked handkerchief and stuffed it into his jacket pocket.

"Let me see," she said, reaching for his hand. "It's stopped bleeding, at least," she said, after she'd examined it. "But you really should clean it up and put some disinfectant on it."

He only shook his head, and withdrew the hand. They sat there for another half hour, not speaking. Morgan continued to drink steadily, smoking one cigarette after another. By the end of the fourth or fifth drink, his eyes were glazing over, and Nora was beginning to worry that he was well on his way to becoming seriously drunk.

He did seem to be more relaxed, however, and he was looking at her now as though really seeing her for the first time.

"Well, how did you like our cozy little family scene?" he said at last in a mocking tone, his voice slightly slurred.

"Not much," she replied, with an encouraging smile. "What was it all about?"

Without giving her a direct answer, he continued speaking in a low monotone. "It's the damned nerve of the old bastard that got to me." He waved his hand in the air, as if to reinforce the point he was making. "It was all his fault. I never did blame her for walking out on us."

He gave her a look of earnest intensity, as though it were extremely important to him to convince her of the truth of what he was saying. "She wanted to stay," he went on, in the same urgent voice. "I know she did. But no woman could be expected to put up with a lazy, drunken bully like him, not even for the sake of her own kids."

He stopped suddenly, and stared down at the drink in his hand. Nora held her breath, not uttering a word, hardly daring to breathe, for fear she'd stop the steady flow of painful memories. It had to be doing him good to get it all out like this.

"I'll never forget the day it happened," he went on. "I was about seven or eight. School was let out early for some damned holiday or other, and she wasn't there when I got home. If you can call that rattrap we lived in 'home.' The ironing board was set up in the kitchen, and she'd already made our dinner. I could smell the soup simmering on the stove. But she was gone." His voice broke. "And she never came back. Never even sent word where she was."

Nora's heart went out to him, yearning to comfort him, to take him in her arms, and tell him it would be all right. But what could she do if he wouldn't let her near him?

Nora's basically practical nature came to her rescue. For a start, she could get him out of here before he made a spectacle of himself. Although he wasn't falling down drunk, he was teetering dangerously on the brink, and was certainly in no condition to make a sensible decision. She'd just have to do it for him.

She rose abruptly to her feet, and pulled on her coat. "Come on, Morgan," she said. "Get up."

He gazed up at her blankly. "What for?"

"It's time to go home." She held out a hand. "Come on."

He scowled, wrinkling his forehead, and continued to stare at her for a few moments, obviously debating. Then, to her intense relief, he finally grasped her hand and levered himself out of his chair. Nora reached for the wallet in her handbag, took out what she hoped would be enough to pay for their drinks, and threw it on the table. Then, she took Morgan firmly by the arm, and guided him out into the street.

At her apartment she debated between making him coffee or getting him straight to bed so he could sleep it off. He'd dozed on the way over in the taxi, and it had been all she could do to rouse him long enough to guide him stumbling up the front stairs.

He seemed quite docile now, sitting on her living-room couch, his knees spread apart, elbows resting on them, his hands clasped before him, staring fixedly down at the floor.

Nora went over and knelt before him. "Morgan," she said, in a low, coaxing voice.

He looked up, and gazed at her, blearily.

"Are you hungry? Would you like something to eat? How about some coffee?"

He shook his head. "No. I don't think so. I'm very tired."

She searched his face. He seemed not so much drunk as exhausted, but at least the pain was gone from his eyes. She stood up, and took him by the hand.

"Come on, then. I'll help you get into bed."

She led him down the hall to her bedroom, and he stood meekly before her while she helped him off with his jacket and tie, undid his shirt, and stripped it off him. Then, she sat him down on the edge of the bed, slipped off his shoes, and pulled his pants down over his long legs.

She pulled the covers aside and he crawled into bed, flopping over on his stomach. She covered him up, and stood gazing down at him. His face was buried in the pillow, his arms flung up over his head, and from the steady rise and fall of his shoulders she could tell that he'd gone to sleep instantly.

She hung up his clothes and turned out the light, then tiptoed quietly out of the room, although by now it would take nothing short of an explosion to rouse him. Wide awake herself, with every sense alert, and suddenly starved, she went into the kitchen to hunt around for something to eat.

She heated a bowl of soup in the microwave, got out cheese and crackers, poured a glass of milk, and sat down at the kitchen table to mull over the strange events of the evening.

She sat there for almost an hour, trying to piece together the disjointed story he'd blurted out at the bar. The intense hatred for his father was understandable now. Apparently, he'd been nothing short of a drunken bully, abusive to the whole family. And Morgan obviously had adored his mother, even though she had left the three children to be raised by that very man. Somehow the story didn't quite fit. There had to be more to it than that.

What was most important to Nora, however, was the fact that the man who had been so maddeningly elusive in the past had finally opened up to her. It had taken a shattering experience and several bourbons to do it, but at last she felt she'd at least caught a glimpse of the real Morgan Latimer beneath the polished, confident veneer.

By the time she'd finished her meal, she was growing drowsy herself. It had been a tiring evening for her, too. She debated calling Anne or Owen to tell them that Morgan was all right and would spend the night with her, but it was past midnight, and they would all have probably gone home long ago.

She cleared away the table, soaked her bowl and utensils in the sink, and went down the hall to the bedroom. Morgan hadn't budged. She undressed in the dark, listening to his deep steady breathing, then crawled into bed beside him, keeping her distance so as not to disturb him.

Wakeful, she lay there for some time, staring up at the dark ceiling, listening to Morgan's steady breathing. Tonight's revelations had brought them so much closer together. She wanted desperately to be there for him, to help him get past the dreadful experiences of his childhood. The love she had already felt for him before now was infused with a deep tenderness, and she'd have to trust in that love to guide her.

Tomorrow, when he was more sober, she would insist on continuing where they'd left off tonight. She couldn't allow him to slip away from her again now that she'd seen the pain that lay behind the mask.

But when she awoke the next morning, he wasn't there. She sat up in bed and darted a look at the closet door, where she'd hung his clothes so carefully the night before. They were gone, too.

She jumped out of bed and ran to the bathroom, the living room, the kitchen. There was no sign that he'd ever even been there. How could she have been so stupid? She should have stayed awake, watched him so he couldn't get away.

She glanced at the clock. It was past nine. Somehow, she had to get to her parents' house in time for Christmas dinner. She didn't know what to do. Last night everything had happened so fast that she hadn't had a chance to ask Morgan to go with her, as she had planned. Maybe it wasn't too late.

She ran to the telephone in the hall, and dialed his number. It rang five times, eight, ten. Still no answer. She slammed the receiver down, and fumbled through the massive Manhattan directory, looking for a number for Owen or Anne.

Of course they weren't listed. But she doubted he would be with either of them, anyway. What if he'd gone back to his place and found his father still there? Visions of bloody mayhem filled her mind, and her first wild thought was to call the police, the hospitals. Better yet, she'd throw on some clothes and make a mad dash over to his place herself.

And do what? Willing herself to be calm, she walked slowly back to the kitchen, where she mechanically went through the motions of making coffee and toast, pouring out a glass of orange juice. The truth was, there was nothing she could do. Morgan wasn't a child. And he wouldn't thank her for making a great to-do over what was probably just a roaring hangover he was sleeping off with the telephone unplugged.

But it was more than a hangover. It wasn't like Morgan to get drunk in the first place. It was something that went far deeper than irritation. She'd never forget the look on his face when his father appeared last night, the sheer hatred on it, as though the devil incarnate had materialized before his eyes.

She mulled over their conversation in the bar. If his mother had left her three children when they were small, and his father had had to raise them alone, surely he deserved some credit. They had all turned out remarkably well. To her way of thinking, the mother who deserted them was the most likely candidate for resentment. Yet he spoke of her as though she'd been some kind of saint. It didn't make sense.

What could the man have done to instill such loathing in his son? The Morgan she knew was the most equable of men, even-tempered, never ruffled by the constant minor aggravations of big-city life, the surly taxi drivers, incompetent waiters, all the daily headaches of managing a multimillion dollar business. He was always so calm, so sure of himself.

Well, she wouldn't know until she talked to him, and it was getting late. It would have to wait. She had promised her parents she'd be there today, and she couldn't let them down. She just had time to get dressed, pack a bag and make the noon train from Grand Central. In the meantime, she'd keep trying to call him from her parents' house.

"Well, Nora," her mother said, some hours later. "Are you going to tell me what's wrong? Or is it none of my business?"

They were doing the dishes in the big old-fashioned kitchen, after an enormous meal of turkey with all the trimmings. Her father had gone upstairs to lie down. He seemed to be feeling better, and in good spirits, but he still tired easily.

Nora gave her mother a wry smile. "I never could fool you for long, could I?"

The older woman busied herself at the sink, scouring the roasting pan in the hot, soapy water. "I was hoping you'd bring your young man with you, today," she said, in a neutral tone.

Nora sighed. "All right, Mother. I'd better tell you the whole story."

As they worked together, she poured out the history of her relationship with Morgan, skipping over the part about the physical side of it in deference to her mother's Victorian sensibilities, but including almost verbatim what had happened the night before.

By the time she'd finished, the dishes were done, and they were sitting across from each other at the table, drinking the remains of the after-dinner coffee. Her mother had listened quietly, never interrupting, only nodding from time to time to let Nora know she was following her, and understood.

Now, she got up from the table and carried her cup to the stove for a refill. "I think there's a great deal you're not telling me, darling," she said, over her shoulder. She came back to the table and stood looking down at her daughter. "Knowing you, it's got to be a much more serious involvement than you let on."

Nora's face went up in flame. She raised her cup to her lips, as if to hide behind it, and remained silent.

"Now, don't worry," her mother said, sitting down and reaching across the table to put her hand over Nora's. "I'm not going to preach. You know my views on the subject." She shook her head. "I don't know what you young people think you have to gain by flaunting the old conventions that were actually designed to protect women, but we won't quibble over that now. The point is, what are you going to do about your situation?"

Suddenly, Nora felt an intense, sickening wave of shame wash over her. If her mother had scolded her, tried to make her feel guilty, it would have been different. But here she was, not uttering a word of judgment, concerned only for her daughter's happiness, and convinced that by indulging in a full-blown affair with Morgan—without even a hint of commitment from him—Nora had actually harmed only herself.

"Well, Mother," she said at last. "There's not a lot I can do about it now. I'm in too deep to back out. What I'm hoping is that he won't clam up on me now that he's finally given me a glimpse of his past life, his true feelings. He was hurting so! There must be something I can do to help him, to make him trust me.''

Her mother shook her head slowly from side to side. ''I hope so, Nora, but I wouldn't count on it. Those wounds run so deep that it will take more than your desire to help to heal them. He's going to have to take a long look at himself first, be willing to face up to his own problems, and stop running away from them or hiding them behind his other successes.''

''But I love him!'' Nora cried. ''Surely that counts for something.''

''Of course it does, darling. It counts for a lot. Love really can heal even the worst wounds. But don't you see? He has to learn to trust in that love first. And that means you must make yourself so vulnerable to him that you risk getting terribly hurt.'' She smiled. ''And as your mother, that's what I want to avoid at all costs.''

For the rest of her stay Nora tried hard to go through the motions of family life for her parents' sake, but all she could think of was getting back to New York, and to Morgan. She called him several times, but there was never a response. She couldn't even leave a message, since he wouldn't have an answering machine, claiming that recording his calls only meant he had to return them.

That was so like him, she thought that night as she tossed and turned in her old narrow bed, and she had to smile. He did things *his* way, and if the world objected it was just too bad.

* * *

The minute she stepped inside her apartment late the next afternoon, she dropped her purse, coat and overnight bag on the floor in the hall, and snatched up the telephone to see if there was a message from him. If not, she was determined to keep calling him until he did answer. And if that didn't work, she'd go to his place and sit outside his door until he showed up. Somehow she would *make* him talk to her.

During the interminable ride back on the train, her mother's words had kept ringing in her ears. She'd been right. Love did mean making oneself vulnerable, taking risks, leaving oneself open to hurt. But it was worth it. And she knew Morgan loved her, at least on some level. All she had to do now was convince him of it.

To her intense relief, there was a message from him on the tape. It was typical Morgan, brief and to the point: "Nora, it's Morgan. Sorry I missed you before you left for Vermont. Call me when you get back."

Quickly, she dialed his number. He certainly sounded perfectly normal. Maybe by now he'd had time to straighten out the mess with his father.

"Hello," came his deep voice.

"Morgan, it's Nora."

"Ah, you're back."

"Yes. I wanted to be with you, but I'd promised my parents I'd spend Christmas Day with them, and couldn't let them down."

He laughed. "Yes, I know. You always keep your promises, don't you?"

"Well, I try. I tried to call you several times yesterday." Keep it light, she warned herself. "I was rather hoping you'd be able to go up there with me. They're dying to meet you.''

"I'm sorry. Actually,'' he went on, in a dry tone, "I wasn't feeling quite up to par, and spent the day nursing the grandfather of all hangovers. I want to apologize about that too, Nora. It couldn't have been very pleasant for you.''

"Oh, don't worry about me. I was just glad I could be there for you.'' She hesitated. "Did you get things settled? I mean about your father.''

"There's nothing to settle,'' he said flatly. The note of finality in his voice was unmistakable. "Now, how about dinner tonight? There's a new Vietnamese restaurant that's just opened in the Village, and I hear the food is quite good.''

They arranged for him to pick her up at the usual time, around seven o'clock. After they'd hung up, Nora picked up her belongings, and walked slowly down the hall to her bedroom. He had shut her out again, and so firmly that she hadn't dared to pursue it. At least, not on the telephone.

As she unpacked, however, she made up her mind that this time she wasn't going to let him get away with it. If love meant taking risks, then it was also a two-way street. Even though he'd never told her he loved her, never made any plans beyond the next dinner date, there was no doubt in her mind that he cared for her.

And the situation wasn't hopeless. Granted, he'd had too much to drink at the time, but at least he *had* revealed his pain to her, and if their static relationship was ever going to move forward he'd have to learn to trust her in the sober light of day, too.

*   *   *

That night, she waited to take the plunge until they'd finished the unusual dinner, so beautifully prepared and presented, and consisting mainly of seafood and exotic vegetables.

They were sipping brandy, and Morgan was sitting back in his chair, relaxed, his eyes half closed, smoking his after-dinner cigarette while they listened to the unfamiliar Oriental music playing softly in the background. He seemed much the same as ever, relaxed, affectionate, chatty, amusing. Although he looked tired, there was little sign of the ravages of what had happened just two nights before, on Christmas Eve, and this gave her courage.

"Morgan," she said.

"Hm?" he said, turning to her with an inquiring look.

She took a deep breath. "Morgan, there's something I'd like to ask you."

He smiled at her. "Ask away."

"Well, we're drifting pretty aimlessly, wouldn't you say?"

He sighed. "Nora, we've been all through that. I've already explained . . ."

"Yes, I know all about your explanations. But they don't make sense." She gathered all her courage. "I have to know, Morgan. Do you really care anything at all about me?"

"Of course I do. In my way," he added carefully.

"Then why do you refuse to make any plans beyond the next dinner date? Why do you clam up when I ask you about your past? Caring means taking risks. I think I've done that. But it's a two-way street. I can't do it alone."

He was silent for a long moment. "What is it you want?" he asked at last.

"Nothing you aren't willing to give. I'm not trying to pin you down to a commitment. But if you keep shutting me out we'll end up just drifting apart. Is that what you want?"

"No," he said swiftly. "All right. What do you want to know?"

She spoke slowly, choosing her words carefully. "The other night you said that your mother had left when you were just a child, and your father had raised the three of you alone. What I don't understand is why he's the one you're so angry at."

She hadn't gone beyond the first tentative words before she could see his expression harden. The smile faded, the gray eyes grew flinty, the firm jaw set in a hard, uncompromising line. Then, as though making an effort to pass it off lightly, he shrugged, and gave her a thin smile.

"It really isn't important, Nora," he said quietly. "Certainly nothing for you to be concerned about."

She leaned across the table and gave him a long, earnest look. "Morgan, everything about you concerns me. Don't you know that by now? I'm not deaf and blind, and to say what happened on Christmas Eve isn't important insults my intelligence. Of course something happened! You were absolutely distraught, almost raving."

"I was drunk," he said tonelessly. "I've already apologized for that, but I'll do it again if it will make you happy."

"It's not a question of my happiness. Don't you see? I just want to help you."

He placed his hands flat on top of the table, and gave her a penetrating look. "I'll say it one more time, Nora. I don't need anyone's help. I don't want it. There's nothing you need to concern yourself about. It has nothing to do with you and me."

She could sense him slipping away from her, retreating into the hard shell, behind the mask again, and this time she wasn't going to let him get away with it. "You're wrong," she said flatly. "It has everything to do with you and me."

His eyes flew open. "Oh? And what does that mean?"

She leaned toward him. "Don't you understand? I—I care very much about you, Morgan. And I think I've proved it in one of the most important ways a woman can."

He flushed. "I know that."

"Then you must also know that whatever affects you, affects me. Whatever *hurts* you, hurts me. If you won't talk about it, you drive a wedge between us." Although she had started out calmly enough, as she went on she could hear her voice rising, the passion throbbing in it, but she couldn't stop herself. "Is that what you want, Morgan? To drive me away? To shut me out of your life?"

"Of course not," was the prompt reply. "It's the last thing I want." He scowled down at his drink, and when he looked up at her again the silvery eyes were softer. "All right. Go on."

Nora wasn't so sure she liked his tone, which sounded an awful lot like a parent humoring an obstreperous child. Still, it was an opening, and she'd better take advantage of it while she had the chance. She settled back in her chair.

"Well, to begin with, while I can understand the bitterness you feel for your father, still it was a long time ago. He's an old man now. I mean, even granting he was everything you say, can't you forgive him?"

"No!" he snapped. "I can't. He was a drunken bully, abusive to the whole family. He made my poor mother's life hell, forced her to run away. I don't want to have anything to do with him."

"Yet Owen and Anne seem to accept him now."

"That's entirely their affair."

"Morgan," she said slowly, "I can't help wondering if there isn't more to it than that. Don't you think your hatred might be harming yourself just as much as it does him?"

His eyes narrowed, and his mouth curled in a mocking smile. "Ah, I didn't know you were a qualified psychologist." He waved a hand airily at her. "But do go on. I find the analysis fascinating."

Nora glared at him, her hackles rising at the sarcastic tone. "All right," she announced coldly, "I will. If your mother left the three of you when you were children, and your father had to raise you alone, surely he deserves some credit. You've all turned out remarkably well, after all. It seems to me that she might be the most likely candidate for resentment, yet you speak of her as though she was some kind of saint."

As she spoke, she could see the color drain out of his face. He was clutching the edge of the table with white-knuckled hands, his mouth pinched, and the gray eyes hard as granite, and looking at her now as though he hated her. With a sinking feeling of dread, she knew she'd gone too far, really trodden on forbidden territory this time.

He just sat there, motionless, for several moments, not saying a word. Finally, he lit a cigarette, took a long swallow of his drink, and the color began to return to his face.

"That's enough of that subject," he said at last. "Just drop it, Nora."

She gazed deep into the silvery eyes. What should she do? He was determined to keep himself hidden from her, and she was only wasting her breath trying to push past defenses she couldn't possibly breach. Not to mention the fact that each probing question only seemed to drive him further away.

"All right," she said resignedly. "If that's the way you want it. I'm sorry," she added stiffly. "I didn't mean to pry."

"It's not a question of prying, Nora. These things are better left alone, that's all. Whatever happened, happened a long time ago. I admit I was disturbed to see him again, but it was the suddenness of it that caught me off guard." He stubbed out his cigarette, and rose out of his chair. "Now, are you ready to leave?"

He was silent and withdrawn on the way back to her apartmemt, sitting well over on his side of the taxi, chin in hand, gazing out of the window, not touching her. Nora sat miserably beside him, wishing now she could take back the things she'd asked him about.

When they reached her place, he got out and held the door open for her, as always. She stepped out on to the pavement and waited for him to follow her, but instead he leaned down to speak to the driver through the open window, before turning to face Nora.

"Sorry, I can't stay. I'm catching an early flight to Paris in the morning."

CHAPTER EIGHT

IN THE days that followed all the light seemed to have gone out of Nora's life. The job that had been so exciting and challenging to her in the past had become merely a matter of going through the motions. What did she care about selling merchandise through clever advertising, beating her brains out to convince an unwary public to buy things they didn't even want?

In time, it even began to seem dishonest to her, a feeling that was somehow linked with the growing suspicion that Morgan had lied to her, that the trip to Paris hadn't even been thought of until that very night, that he'd dreamed it up on the spur of the moment.

It took all her willpower not to call his office, or try to get in touch with Anne or Owen, to find out just what was going on. What good would it do to humiliate herself by chasing a man who seemed to be avoiding her?

It was the middle of January now, and one cold evening Nora stood at the window of her living room looking down at the remains of the December snowfall, still piled up at the curbs of the city streets, the dirty gray, icy masses gleaming dully in the light from the street lamp.

The depressing sight didn't do much to lift her glum spirits, and when the telephone rang she was glad of the interruption. When she answered, and heard Morgan's voice, relief flooded through her.

"You're back!" she cried happily. "How was the trip?"

"Pretty dull. Business mostly."

"It must have been hectic for you."

"Not really. Why?"

She fought down a spurt of irritation at his offhand manner, and laughed to cover it up. "Well, after all, I haven't heard a word from you for over two weeks, not even a postcard."

"Not much point in that, since I knew I'd be back before you received it."

"I assume Europe has telephone service," she retorted sharply. "And I don't think you're exactly unable to afford such luxuries as transatlantic telephone calls." He was silent for so long that she began to wonder if the line hadn't gone dead. "Morgan?" she said. "Are you there?"

"Yes," he replied. "Listen, if you're not busy I'd like to come over."

"No, I'm not busy. Just give me half an hour to get organized. I've been working such long hours lately that I'm afraid the place is in a mess."

After they hung up, she raced around picking up the litter she'd been too self-absorbed to clear away lately, the magazines and newspapers that had piled up, her heavy coat, bag, and briefcase still on the chair where she'd left them when she came home from work, her shoes still on the floor just inside the door.

She ran into the bedroom, and threw up her hands at the mess inside. However, she didn't have time to worry about that now. There was a far more pressing problem. She peered into the mirror, and ran her hands through her hair. It hadn't been styled for over a week, and she'd just pulled it back carelessly behind her ears that morning. She was wearing an old torn pair of jeans and a wrinkled, faded pink sweatshirt. At least she'd already had her shower.

There was no time for a complete overhaul. She'd just have to do her best. Tearing off her clothes, she slipped into a long velvet hostess gown, a lovely shade of royal blue that Morgan particularly liked, and a pair of low-heeled matching slippers. She brushed her hair vigorously until it shone, then pinned it as best she could in a rough approximation of the way the hairdresser usually styled it.

When the doorbell rang, she just had time to powder her nose and dab on a dash of pale lipstick. With one last agonizing glance at the clutter in the bedroom, she switched off the light, ran down the hall to the front door, and threw it open.

He looked wonderful, his face slightly reddened from the cold, the collar of his heavy coat pulled up around the back of his neck, his dark hair neatly brushed. She started toward him, longing to feel his arms around her, but before she could take a step he had already brushed past her, and was standing inside taking off his coat.

"I'll hang that up for you," she said, moving closer to him.

"Never mind," he replied, throwing it over a chair. "I can't stay long."

She stopped short. Something about his tone of voice, the way he was not quite looking at her, his whole posture, warned her that this was not going to be the happy homecoming she had anticipated.

With her heart in her mouth, she went to his side, and smiled up at him. "Well, then, can I get you something? Coffee? A drink?"

"No, thanks." He reached out to take her loosely by the arm. "Can we sit down? I have something to say to you."

"Of course."

When they were seated at either end of the long couch in front of the fireplace, he clasped his hands between his knees and gazed down at the carpet for a few seconds, then turned to her, his face grave. She waited, her heart thudding heavily.

"While I was gone," he began slowly, "I did a lot of thinking. About us."

She gave him a tremulous smile. "That sounds like very serious thinking," she said brightly. "What was your conclusion?"

"I think," he said carefully, "that we shouldn't see each other any more."

Nora felt as though all her muscles had suddenly become paralyzed, the smile still frozen on her face. Her mind simply went blank. She'd been afraid of this, but now that her worst fears were a reality, she couldn't think, couldn't make herself function.

"I see," she said at last. "Do you mind telling me why?"

He got up and walked over to the fireplace, and stood staring down at the dead coals inside the grate for a few moments, then turned slowly around to face her.

"Believe it or not," he said in a distant voice, "I'm thinking mainly of you."

Nothing he could have said would have irritated her more. "And just what does that mean?" she bit out.

He shrugged. "It means that you're too fine a person to waste your time on a man who has nothing to offer you." He waved a hand in the air. "I mean, I hoped I'd made it clear from the beginning of our—our relationship that any serious commitment was out of the question for me. At least that was my intention."

Although Nora was inwardly shattered at this sudden turn of events, the cold withdrawal, the hurtful words, as she listened to him, she grew angrier with each passing second.

Finally, she rose to her feet and walked over to him, her hands clenched at her sides, her eyes blazing. "And just what gives you the right to decide all this on your own, without even discussing it with me?" He opened his mouth to speak, but she hadn't finished yet. "After two weeks of my not hearing one word from you, you suddenly show up here and calmly announce that you want out. And I want to know why. I think I have that right."

"Yes, you do," he said stiffly. "I thought I already explained that. I just decided that I had no right to tie you to a situation that isn't going anywhere. You deserve better than that."

"*You* decided," she said, in a low voice that dripped with sarcasm. "That's very considerate of you. And the fact that I got a little too close to you after that scene with your father on Christmas Eve has nothing to do with it."

His eyes flew open. "Of course not."

"I see. Then you've simply decided you want to go on now to greener pastures, is that it?"

He scowled darkly at her. "No, that's not it," he snapped. Then his face softened. "Please, Nora, let's not have a scene. These things just happen, that's all."

It was then she knew it was hopeless. She was certain he was lying to her. Or what was even worse, lying to himself. It didn't matter. She was suddenly filled with a terrible sense of defeat, a deep lethargy.

"I just have one thing to say to you, Morgan," she said at last. "And then I want you to go. In the beginning, I was all prepared to be a one-night stand, at most a brief fling. I wasn't crazy about the idea; it's not my style at all, and you knew it."

"Yes," he muttered. "I knew that. But——"

She held up a hand. "No. Let me finish. I'm not blaming you for that. I went into it with my eyes open, and take full responsibility for my own actions. But what I can't forgive you for is that you led me to believe you cared for me."

"I *do* care for you!" he exclaimed. "That's why—— " He broke off and turned his head away. "I do care," he repeated. "In my way. I think you're a wonderful person, and some day a man is going to come along who will give you what you want, what you deserve. It's just not going to be me. I can't get involved."

"But you *are* involved!" she cried. She could feel the tears stinging behind her eyes. In another moment she'd start to cry, and that was the last thing she wanted to do. It was over. There was no changing his mind. If he wanted to think he was doing this for her sake, then let him.

Before he could say another word, she marched over to the chair where he'd left his coat, picked it up, and held it out to him. "Will you please leave now?"

He stood there by the fireplace a few moments longer, gazing down at the floor, as though suddenly reluctant to go. And even in her distress, Nora had the impression that he was hurting, too. Maybe she was giving in too easily. She loved him, she believed that on some level, at least, he loved her. Should she fight for him?

But it was too late for that. He raised his head, took his coat from her, and paused a moment. She held her breath, still fighting back the tears she couldn't let him see, refusing to meet his eyes. Then she heard his footsteps heading for the door. It opened and shut, and when she looked up again he was gone.

During the next few awful days, Nora couldn't get the haunting memory of that last look he'd given her out of her mind. If only she could have believed he was just a callous playboy who had wined her, dined her, flattered her, seduced her, then dumped her when it began to get serious, it wouldn't have been so bad.

She'd suspected from the beginning that she was playing with fire, but had gone ahead, anyway, and now she had only herself to blame. She'd been a little more than a one-night stand to him, but not an awful lot.

She thought about all those expensive clothes she'd bought to dazzle him, make him think she was something she wasn't, the makeup, the sophisticated hairstyles. She'd turned herself into an artificial doll to attract him, to keep him interested in her.

Finally, as a kind of symbolic act of purification, she went to her bedroom one rainy Sunday afternoon, and took all the new dresses out of the cupboard, along with the high-heeled shoes that had been so uncomfortable, and piled them in a carton. She left hanging a few of the more tailored suits and blouses that she could still wear to work, but all the rest she stowed away at the back of the linen cupboard in the hall. The bottles and jars of makeup were next, then the lacy lingerie, the frothy nightgowns and silky underclothes she'd bought just for him.

As she was going through the dresser drawers, ruthlessly removing every last trace of the false image she'd worked so hard to project for his sake, her eye fell on the jeweler's box he'd given her at Christmas, the diamond pendant still inside. She opened it and stared down at the sparkling gems, the thin gold chain. She'd never wear it again. Quickly, before she could get maudlin about it, she snapped the lid shut and put it in the carton with the makeup.

After that ritual she actually did feel better, somehow cleaner, less cheapened by the whole affair. She'd been a fool, of course, and still felt like one, but, she hoped, a little wiser.

What saved her in the end was her work, and she threw herself into the latest ad campaign as though her life depended on it. It was early March now, almost two months since she'd broken up with Morgan. The winter's accumulation of snow had finally melted, and soon it would be spring, the season of lovers.

It was the first really bright sunny day, and during her lunch hour she'd gone for a short walk in Central Park. The daffodils and hyacinths were in full bloom, the trees already beginning to show bright traces of green, and every path seemed to be swarming with couples, strolling along in the sunshine, their arms around each other, basking in the joy of just being alive and together on such a fine day.

It was more than she could bear, and after twenty minutes of it she turned her steps resolutely back to the agency. Even after all this time she kept looking for Morgan on every street corner, at every turn of the winding paths. There was no escaping it. Only in her office, absorbed in her work, was she free of that aching void in her heart that it seemed would go on forever.

She had just settled herself behind her desk, trying to work up an interest in the new project, when Jerry suddenly burst inside in his usual slapdash, noisy manner. She hadn't seen him for a few weeks, and was glad of the interruption. His zany sense of humor always gave her a lift.

"Nora," he called, waving a heavy cardboard portfolio at her, "I just got the proofs for the cosmetic ad. Want to take a look at them?"

She smiled up at him and reached out a hand. "Sure. How did they turn out?"

He was walking slowly towards her now, staring at her intently, a puzzled look on his face. "Say, what's happened to the glamour girl I've enjoyed looking at so much for the past few months?''

Nora ran a hand over her hair, uncut for several weeks and pinned back in the familiar untidy bun, then glanced down at the old brown suit. Since cleaning out her cupboard a few weeks ago, she'd slipped naturally into her old habits of dressing and grooming.

She grinned at Jerry, amused by the look of dismay on his face. ''Is it that bad?''

''No,'' he replied slowly, running his eyes over her. ''As a matter of fact, if the truth were known I felt a hell of a lot more comfortable with the way you looked before—um...'' His voice trailed off, and he shrugged offhandedly. Then he perched on the edge of her desk, and gazed down at her. ''I don't mean to tread on forbidden territory,'' he said carefully, ''but I take it you and Latimer are no longer an item.''

It had to come sooner or later. Even the normally outspoken Gloria had been tiptoeing around her as though walking on eggs, never mentioning Morgan's name, never quizzing her about the status of the relationship, shooting her sympathetic looks as though she were recovering from a terrible illness.

''Yes, Jerry,'' she said, as cheerfully as possible. ''You take it correctly.'' She reached out a hand. ''Now let's take a look at those proofs. We have an April the first deadline.''

Jerry took the eight by ten glossies out of the portfolio, and after he'd set them out on top of her desk they spent the next hour choosing which photographs would be most appropriate for the proposed magazine layout.

At two o'clock, Robert McKenzie appeared at the door. "Do you have a minute, Nora?" he said. He gestured toward the display on her desk. "Oh, it looks like you're pretty involved right now."

Jerry slid off the desk, and started gathering up the photos. "No, sir," he said. "We've just finished." He glanced at Nora. "So, are we agreed on these four, then?"

"Right, Jerry. They're wonderful, just what I wanted."

When he was gone, McKenzie closed the door behind him and came back to sit down in the chair opposite Nora's desk. He looked quite pleased with himself and was beaming at her, his broad face creased in a smile of intense satisfaction.

"Well, Nora, it looks as though you've gathered another nice big plum for the agency."

"Oh? What's that?"

The smile widened, the blue eyes twinkled, and he leaned closer to her with an almost conspiratorial air. "Latimer's want us to do a television commercial for them. What's more, they're insisting that you produce it."

Nora's heart flipped over, then simply stopped beating for a few seconds. It occurred to her that this was practically the first time she'd even heard his name mentioned since the breakup. She stared at her boss as though he'd just issued an order for her execution.

"I'm sorry," she said stiffly at last. "I can't do that."

His eyes flew open, then narrowed as his expression hardened. "Why the devil not?"

She shrugged helplessly. "I just can't. It's not my line of expertise. I don't have the background for television."

"Nonsense!" he exclaimed. "That toy commercial you did last autumn was a rousing success."

"That was different."

"How different?"

She knew he wasn't going to let it go. If one of the agency's biggest clients was prepared to spend thousands on a television commercial, and had asked specifically for her, there was simply no way out of it.

"You said they want me for the job," she said finally, in a cautious voice. "Was it anyone in particular?"

He frowned, puzzled. "I don't see what difference that makes, but as I recall it was Morgan Latimer himself."

Her heart sank. What was he doing, throwing her a bone? I don't love you, don't want you in my life, but I'll help you in your career. Then the irony of it hit her. It was what he had proposed to her the first night they'd had dinner together. Surely he wasn't going to use that old ploy to get her back in his bed?

In the end, of course, she had to agree to do it. It was either that or write off her career at the McKenzie agency. Not only that, but it was the professional thing to do. If Morgan did have a personal motive in this totally unexpected move, it was no concern of hers. She'd do her best for him, but only as a valued client. Her personal feelings didn't enter into it at all, and there was no reason for her to deal with him directly, in any event.

* * *

As it turned out, she needn't have worried. The commercial wasn't scheduled to appear on the air until the autumn, and that meant several months of preliminary work, deciding on a central theme, coming up with catchy phrases to attract the viewer, writing the content, interviewing models, a seemingly endless stream of decisions to be made, and the whole thing fell on her shoulders.

During this stage of the operation there was no need for any interaction whatever with Latimer's. McKenzie took care of the business end, and, while it was entirely possible that Morgan might show up in the agency's offices from time to time for practical discussions of that nature, there was no reason for her to even see him. Unless by a fluke, as on that first occasion when she'd mistaken him for a model.

She also had other projects to keep her busy, mainly the cosmetics ad that was to appear in June issues of the leading fashion magazines. She worked long hours, even spending her weekends doing what she could at home, so that the days flew by, and it was only in the darkest hours of the night, when she was lying sleepless in the dark that she would remember what she'd once had—and lost.

Soon it was May, the loveliest time of year in the city, and the Latimer's commercial was coming along quite nicely, with none of the usual hitches and hassles that could occur. All the important decisions had been made, and from now on it would only be a matter of filling in the gaps until they were ready to start shooting, in late August.

In all that time, Nora hadn't seen Morgan once. At first she'd cast a wary eye up and down the hallways before venturing out of her office, worried that he might be there, but by now she was confident that even if they did meet accidentally she would be able to handle it.

So that when she finally did see him she was totally unprepared for it. It was on one of those unpredictable spring days that started out fair and sunny with a cloudless blue sky, then turned to showers by afternoon. Nora had just come back from a meeting at the cosmetics firm and been caught on her way in the downpour, without an umbrella or a raincoat.

She stepped out of the elevator, dripping wet, and the first thing she saw in the waiting room was Morgan. He was standing at the window, his hands stuck in his pant pockets, looking out at the rain pelting against it. His back was toward her, but she would have recognized the tall form, the graceful athletic posture, the dark head, anywhere.

In spite of herself, memories came flooding back. The first time she'd ever seen him had been in this exact spot, under almost the exact same circumstances. Not quite, however. Then they had no history together. Now they did, and it wasn't pleasant.

Her first instinct was to run, but it was too late. In that split second of indecision he'd turned and seen her, stared intently at her for a moment, and was now approaching her, slowly. Of all the times for them to run into each other! she agonized, when she looked like nothing in the world so much as a drowned rat. She ran a nervous hand over her wet hair and stood her ground, waiting until he stopped just a few feet away.

"Hello, Nora," he said gravely. "It's been a while."

Now that he was so close and she had a good look at him, she was so shocked by his appearance that she forgot all about her own jangled nerves. He looked as though he'd been ill, his face drawn and haggard, the dark hair lifeless and a little too long, the old lift to his shoulders gone.

She forced out a thin smile. "Hello, Morgan."

She gave him a curt nod and was just about to walk past him, when Robert McKenzie came into the room, making straight for them, a broad smile on his smooth bland face, his hand outstretched to Morgan.

"Ah, Latimer," he said. "Sorry to keep you waiting." He glanced at Nora. "But I see Nora has filled the gap. I suppose you two have a lot to talk about." Suddenly, he broke into a loud chuckle. "Hope she hasn't tried to enlist you as a model this time," he said heartily. "That wasn't the most auspicious introduction."

The smile on Nora's face felt frozen in place. Her facial muscles were beginning to ache, and her back teeth were clamped together.

"Well," she finally managed to stammer, "as you can see, I got caught in the rain and had better go and get dried off." She turned to Morgan. "It was nice to see you again, Mr. Latimer."

She walked away from the two men, willing herself to walk slowly, her head high, all the while conscious that she was probably dripping water on the carpet the entire distance. When she finally turned the corner and was safely out of their sight, she made a dash for her office. Once inside, she shut the door behind her, leaned back against it, her eyes closed, and uttered a silent, heartfelt prayer of gratitude that it was over.

When she opened her eyes she saw Gloria standing in the doorway to the adjoining room, staring at her. "What in the world happened to you?" she asked.

Nora shook herself. "As you can see, I got caught in the rain," she replied briskly. "I don't suppose you could find a towel for me, do you? Then I want you to help me organize the notes I took at the meeting with the cosmetics people this afternoon."

Half an hour later, dried off, her hair combed and pinned back, Nora was dictating to Gloria when she was interrupted in the middle of a sentence by a light rapping on the door.

"Come in," she called.

The door opened, and Morgan stepped inside. He darted a quick glance at Gloria, then smiled and nodded at her. "Hello. It's Gloria, isn't it?"

"Yes," Gloria replied, actually blushing, and obviously thrilled out of her mind that he'd remembered her.

He came up to the desk. "Gloria, would you mind giving me a few minutes alone with Nora?"

Gloria jumped immediately to her feet. "No, of course not." She grabbed her notebook and pencil, and hurried past him into the hallway, closing the door quietly behind her.

When she was gone, Morgan stood there for a while, not saying anything. Nora's mind was in a turmoil. She was irritated by the way he'd ordered *her* assistant around, apprehensive at being alone with him like this, and intensely curious as to why he'd maneuvered her into this awkward situation in the first place.

Finally, the silence became unbearable. She couldn't tolerate another minute of it. She got up, and stood glaring at him across the desk.

"I don't know what you want, Morgan," she said, in a low voice, "but unless it has to do with the work I'm doing for Latimer's I don't see that we have anything to talk about."

He gazed at her rather blankly, as though he hadn't heard a word she'd said. "How have you been, Nora?" he asked at last.

"I've been fine," she retorted. "What did you expect? That I'd have gone into a decline after you dumped me?" She could have bitten her tongue out the moment the petty, childish words escaped her lips.

He winced visibly. "That's not an entirely accurate description of what happened."

She shrugged wearily. "All right. Have it your way. It doesn't matter in the slightest. Now, would you please tell me what it is you want? I have a lot of work to do."

"May I sit down?" he asked.

She hesitated for a moment, then decided that since he was the client, after all, she should be civil to him just for the sake of the agency. She nodded curtly, sat back down in her own chair, then folded her hands on top of the desk in front of her, and waited.

"I guess most of all I want to apologize," he said, after seating himself opposite her. "The last time we met I handled things very badly, and it's preyed on my mind ever since.''

"Morgan," she broke in impatiently, "whatever happened was inevitable. I admit I was hurt at the time." She laughed shortly. "I still had a few illusions, then, romantic pipe dreams, if you will. We had a good time together, and if I took it more seriously than you intended I can still chalk it up to experience. It was a valuable lesson for me.''

He stared bleakly at her for several seconds. "You've changed," he stated flatly at last.

"I sincerely hope so," she said, with feeling.

He shook his head. "I don't mean the essential person. That will never change. I mean, you look so different.''

"Well, I did get caught out in the rain, after all.''

"No, it's more than that." He gazed at her, examining her as though she were under a microscope. "I know what it is. You look much the same as you did the first day we met.''

"Yes, I was drenched that day, too." She laughed lightly. "I seem to make a habit of it. Anyway," she went on briskly, "you didn't come here to discuss my appearance. You've said what you had to say. There was no need to apologize, but if it makes you feel any better, the apology is accepted. No hard feelings. Now, if that's all——''

"Don't!" he broke in loudly. Then, in a softer tone, "Don't shut me out like that. Please.''

Startled at the sudden interruption, she could only gaze blankly at him, speechless. Then, in a sudden abrupt movement, he got up from his chair, rocking it so that it almost fell over. He rested his hands flat on her desk, and leaned over it toward her, fixing her with glinting gray eyes.

"I know I have no right to ask this, Nora," he said quietly. "But I want another chance with you."

CHAPTER NINE

NORA'S mouth fell open, and she sat there staring at him for a good ten seconds. The room began to spin, the contours of his face seemed to be swimming before her eyes. Had she heard him right? Surely not. Morgan Latimer was the last man in the world to humble himself this way for a woman.

His eyes never left hers. "Will you?" he said. "Give me another chance?"

She leapt to her feet so abruptly that a pile of folders on the edge of her desk slid to the floor. "No!" she cried. She bent over to pick up the folders, and sat back down again. "That's not possible," she went on in a quieter voice. "Surely you can see that it wouldn't work?"

"Before you give me a definite answer, perhaps I'd better explain a few things, then we can discuss it."

"But I *have* given you a definite answer!" she said. "There's nothing to discuss."

"Five minutes," he ground out. "That's all I ask."

Now that she'd taken it in that she had heard him right, that he really meant what he'd said, she felt a little calmer. Her heart was still pounding, and she felt very warm, but her vision had cleared so that she could see now from the expression on his face just how much this was costing him, and she felt herself softening toward him.

She shook her head slowly from side to side. "Morgan," she said, in a low voice, "if you only knew how hard it's been for me to get over you, you wouldn't ask such a question. I can't go back to the way things were between us. It's simply not possible."

"I'm not asking you to do that." He got up out of his chair, and came around the desk to stand beside her. "That's what I want to talk to you about. I was wrong; I was unfair to you. Won't you just listen?"

In spite of all the warning bells in her head, the almost certain knowledge that even listening to what he had to say would only mean more hurt for her ahead, she couldn't help herself. She thought she'd got over him. Now she knew she still loved him.

She finally nodded her acquiescence. "All right," she said. "Five minutes."

He walked over to the window and stood looking out for a few moments. It had stopped raining, and a pale sun glittered through the drops still clinging to the windowpane. Finally, he turned around, leaned his narrow hips back against the sill, and folded his arms across his chest.

"Until you came along," he began quietly, "I was quite content with my life just the way it was. I had decided very early on that a serious commitment to a woman was out of the question for me. There were reasons, and I think you have an idea what they were, but that isn't important now."

At that point it was all she could do to keep from jumping up and screaming at him that they damned well *were* important, but she'd promised she'd listen for five minutes, and she clamped her jaw shut hard so that she wouldn't be able speak.

"Anyway," he went on, "you get the picture." He gave her a crooked smile. "Then I met you. At first I was intrigued by the fact that you were different from all the other women I'd known. That first day we met when you thought I was a model made a strong impression on me. You were so professional, so natural, so sincere. There was no artifice about you at all, and I liked that."

He came back and sat down again. "Then, when I called that first time and asked you to have dinner with me, and you wouldn't go because you'd already made a promise to your family, I was doubly impressed, with your honesty, your loyalty to your commitments. However, as I told you, I had to go to Paris the next week, and I forgot about the whole episode." He shrugged. "There was the pressure of business, of course, but I was also in the process of extricating myself from another..." he paused "...another involvement," he finally added.

He gazed at her for a moment, the gray eyes softly alight. "Then when I saw you at the party that night, and you looked so spectacular in that lovely green dress, I forgot all about the girl I'd met in the office who had intrigued me so." He shrugged, a little shamefaced. "Quite simply, I wanted you. And, I'm afraid, from your manner, your whole rather seductive appearance, I simply assumed you were available."

Nora's cheeks burned. "That wasn't really me," she muttered. "I don't know what I could have been thinking of. I guess," she added carefully, "I continued the charade after that mainly because you seemed to like it."

He leaned forward. "But that's only the way it started out," he said eagerly. "I admit I was attracted by the facade, but as I came to know the real person underneath the sophisticated trappings it was you I fell in love with."

Nora's eyes widened. "You never told me that," she whispered.

"No. I was afraid to. Afraid of commitment, I guess. But now, having lost you, I find I can't live without you. I've been brooding over this for some time, missing you, kicking myself for not hanging on to you, but today, when I saw you get out of the elevator looking like a half-drowned kitten, it hit me. It's *you* I love, Nora, *you* I want to marry."

Nora sucked in a deep breath. Every nerve in her body was tingling. Morgan loved her, wanted to marry her. A great surge of happiness flooded through her. She was just about to get up and run to him, when something stopped her, a nagging little doubt, something that had to be resolved before she could take what he was offering her.

"Morgan, there's something I have to know."

"Anything," he replied swiftly.

"Your unwillingness to commit yourself was only part of the problem between us. I felt that you backed away from me not so much because of that, but because I got too close to you. Remember that night your father showed up at your place, Christmas Eve?"

"How could I ever forget?" he muttered. "I made quite a spectacle of myself. Listen, if it's drinking that worries you, that was strictly a one-time occurrence. It won't happen again.''

Nora waved a hand dismissively in the air, and frowned. ''No, of course not. I know you're not a heavy drinker. What concerns me is that while you were under the influence you talked about your childhood for the first time, and I could see that something so terrible had happened to you that you'd never quite got over it. Then, later, when I broached the subject, you backed off, shut me out.''

''But it's not important,'' he said. ''It's all in the past. What matters is the present, the future, you and me, together.''

''I don't think so,'' she said slowly. ''Just tell me one thing. Have you made it up with your father?''

''No,'' he said shortly. ''And I don't expect to.''

The closed-in look was back on his face. Nora's heart sank. Whatever troubled Morgan about his past would affect their future. It wasn't so much that he was hiding his feelings from her, but from himself. It would always be between them.

But maybe she had to take that chance. Maybe her love would heal the wounds that shadowed his life. She gazed at him, searching his face for an answer. But the well-remembered mask was firmly in place. She'd never be able to penetrate that. Still, she had to try one more time.

''Will you tell me about it now?'' she asked softly.

His jaw was set, his eyes narrowed at her. ''There's nothing to tell.'' Then his gaze softened. ''Believe me, Nora, it has no bearing whatsoever on the way I feel about you.''

She wanted to believe him, to drop the whole subject that was obviously so painful to him, but she couldn't do that. "Will you at least tell me what happened?" she persisted. "I guess what I don't understand is why you despise your father so much when it was your mother who ran out on you."

A dark red flush washed over his face, and he rose to his feet. "I came here today to ask you to give me another chance, not to discuss my family. I was perfectly willing to admit that I did all the taking, while you did all the giving. Isn't that enough? Why the sudden inquisition?"

She could feel him slipping away from her, virtually see the barriers he was erecting, and she was filled with a dull ache that seemed to penetrate to her very bones. She rose slowly to her feet, and gazed sadly at him.

"I'm sorry, Morgan," she said. "But so long as you're determined to keep the most important part of yourself hidden from me, I don't see that we have any future together."

He opened his mouth, as though to argue with her, hesitated for a moment, then gave her one abrupt nod, turned on his heel, and stalked out of the room.

When he was gone, Nora sat back down and put her head in her hands. This was worse, far worse, than before. Losing him a second time was more than she could bear.

Had she been a complete idiot? Maybe he was right. His past was his own business. She had no right to pry into it when he was so insistent that it had no bearing on their relationship. He'd said he loved her, wanted to marry her. What more did she want?

She half rose out of her chair, ready to run after him. It wasn't too late. Then she saw again that look on his face when she touched upon the part his mother had played in his childhood drama, the look that said "No Trespassing" in giant letters. What kind of life could they have together when there were vast areas inside him that she didn't dare touch upon?

She'd got over him once, and she could do it again. She had no choice.

She didn't see him or hear from him again, nor had she expected to. The lonely weeks dragged on. It was late July now, the height of summer. Soon they'd start shooting the Latimer's commercial, and she still had to choose a model, preferably one with acting experience, since there would be lines to speak.

One hot, muggy afternoon, after what seemed like the millionth interview with one unsuitable candidate after another, Nora was at the door of her office, on her way to the studio to consult with Jerry about the one promising screen test he'd made a few days ago, when the telephone on her desk rang. She called out, asking Gloria to answer it, but then remembered she'd already left for a late lunch.

Muttering under her breath, she crossed over to the desk, and snatched up the receiver. "Nora Graham," she said curtly.

"Nora," came the woman's voice. "This is Anne Latimer, Morgan's sister. I don't know if you remember me, since we only met a few times, some months ago.''

Nora sat down on her chair. "Of course I remember you, Anne. What can I do for you?"

"I'd like to talk to you. Do you suppose we could meet for a drink after work, this evening?"

Nora's first instinct was to refuse. She wanted nothing to do with any member of the Latimer family. But she had liked Anne, who seemed to have a practical, no-nonsense approach to life that was very much like her own. Besides, even though she wasn't that active in the business, she was the client.

"All right," she said at last. "I'll probably be working late, however, and won't be able to get away until seven. Is that all right?"

"Fine," Anne agreed. "Shall we meet at the bar in the Algonquin Hotel? That's fairly close to your office."

After they'd hung up, Nora sat there staring into space for several moments, her hand still on the receiver. What in the world could Anne Latimer want with her? Had something happened to Morgan? She firmly dismissed the thought. It was none of her business. He'd made that perfectly clear.

The Algonquin bar was always crowded, but especially so in the early hours of the evening. It was an old-fashioned hotel, with a lot of interesting history behind it, having once been the scene of the famous writers' Round Table in the thirties. Nowadays, it was patronized more by business people—stockbrokers, lawyers, and advertising executives—than by artists.

Nora craned her neck, looking for Anne at the long wooden bar. Every stool was occupied, with waiting customers two deep behind those lucky enough to have found a seat. There was no sign of Anne, but then, above the din, she heard someone call her name. She turned to see her sitting at a small table over by the window, and made her way through the crowd toward it.

"I'd forgotten how jammed this place is," Anne said, when Nora was seated across from her. "I ordered a carafe of white wine. I hope that's all right."

"Fine," Nora replied. "That's about all I drink, anyway."

Anne filled a glass for her, and the two women sat sipping the cold wine for a few minutes, commenting on the hot weather and the progress of the Latimer's commercial.

Finally, Anne drained the last of the wine in her glass, and gave Nora a tentative smile. "I suppose you're wondering why I called and asked you to meet me this evening."

Nora returned the smile. "Well, it did cross my mind."

"It's about Morgan."

Nora stiffened. In the back of her mind she'd been afraid of that; in fact, she couldn't think of another reason why his sister would want to talk to her, but now that it was actually out in the open, with no way to avoid it, she wished she hadn't come at all. She also wondered just how much Morgan had told her about their last meeting. Knowing him, it couldn't have been very much.

"He'd kill me," Anne was going on, "if he knew I'd done this, but in spite of all his failings, his stubbornness, his stupid refusal to face facts, I love *both* my brothers very much. Morgan, especially, I suppose, since he's more vulnerable." She smiled. "Odd, isn't it, since Owen is the artistic one, and supposed to be sensitive? But it's always been Morgan I've worried about the most, because he was far more attached to our mother than Owen or I were."

Nora's ears pricked up at that, but she reminded herself that it was not her affair any longer. "Forgive me, Anne," she said. "But why are you telling me this?"

"Because I can't stand to see him hurting the way he's been ever since you turned him down." She waved a hand in the air. "Oh, he hasn't spelled it out for me. Morgan never would. But from his evasive replies to a few cautious questions I think I get the picture." She sighed. "I always knew he'd fall one day, and when he did it would be a disaster for him."

Nora bridled at that. "Are you blaming me for what happened then?"

"Oh, no," Anne hastily assured her. "Not at all. It's just that it's natural for a woman to want to know what makes the man she loves tick, and I knew Morgan would never reveal the deepest part of himself, the part that hurts him the most. You see, he's always had this fantasy that our mother left us because Dad was so cruel, even abusive."

"And was he?" Nora asked, fascinated, in spite of herself.

Anne shrugged. "Well, I'll have to admit he wasn't a model husband or father." She smiled. "Actually, he was hardest on Morgan because he was his favorite. I think he had some idea of reliving his wasted life through him."

"And your mother never returned?"

Anne shook her head. "Nope. Never even wrote us a postcard."

"Why did she leave, then?"

"Simple. She had a lover and ran off with him. Oh, I'm not saying the old man didn't give her good cause. He was a weak man. He drank too much, couldn't hold a job for long."

"And Morgan's fantasy about her?"

"Well, as I said, Morgan was the sensitive one. He adored our mother, and when she left what else could he do but blame Dad?"

"Thanks for telling me all this, Anne," Nora said at last. "It helps me to understand better what went wrong between us. But I can't see what difference it makes now. I did my best to get Morgan to open up to me, but I came up against a blank wall every time. I just don't see that there's anything more I can do."

"Let me ask you one question. Do you love Morgan?"

Nora reddened, and looked away. "I did," she said slowly. "I guess some part of me still does."

"Then what I wanted to ask you, to beg you, was not to give up on him. You were dead right to keep trying to make him open up, and I think he loves you enough so that eventually he would have done it rather than lose you. But now, without any hope of getting you back, I'm afraid he will never come to terms with the past. It's selfish, I know, but there's so much good in Morgan, and I think with the right woman—with you, Nora—he'd make a fine husband. Won't you try?''

"Believe me, Anne, I have tried. But it would take a miracle to get past those barriers.''

Anne nodded vigorously. "I know that. But if you could take just one more shot at it, I think it might work. He really is hurting, Nora.''

Nora sighed. "What do you want me to do?''

"Whatever your heart tells you to do. I'm not saying it would be easy. It would mean making yourself vulnerable to him, and yet forcing him to face these issues at the same time—a tricky business. But I think you could handle it, if you love him enough.''

"I don't know, Anne. I'll have to think about it.''

"That's all I ask.'' She began to gather up her things. "I'd better get home. The monsters will be screaming for Mommy.'' She got up, and put a hand on Nora's shoulder as she passed by. "Thanks for listening, anyway.'' She gave the shoulder a squeeze. "And miracles have been known to happen.''

When she was gone, Nora sat there for half an hour, finishing her wine and thinking over the strange conversation. It shed so much light on Morgan's stubborn resistance to discuss his past. She felt she understood him much better. But what was she going to do about it?

It was still light outside when she left the hotel, although the summer sun had already dipped below the tall skyscrapers to the west, casting dark shadows on the caverns below.

She wasn't hungry, and she didn't want to go home just yet to the lonely, empty apartment that had seemed like a prison to her ever since that last night Morgan had spent there with her. It seemed like ages ago, yet in another way it could have been yesterday.

She walked the city streets, block after block, her mind in a turmoil, wondering what, if anything, she was going to do about the revelations Anne had made to her.

It was interesting that both her own mother and Anne Latimer had said pretty much the same thing to her, not only that Morgan did need to learn to deal with what was hurting him, but also that if she loved him she must help him, risk getting hurt herself, even another rejection.

It had been two months since that last talk they'd had in her office. She hadn't needed to send him away so finally. Couldn't she have handled things better, treated him more gently, not given up quite so quickly? Her own ego had been wounded by his rejection, and perhaps a part of her wanted to hurt him the way he'd hurt her, had even enjoyed seeing him crawl.

Finally, after walking for what seemed like miles, and getting nowhere closer to a decision, she began to feel definite pangs of hunger gnawing at her stomach. She was only a few blocks away from her apartment by now, but there was nothing edible in the kitchen cupboards at home except a few cans of soup.

She turned into the McDonald's on the corner, and guiltily ordered a Big Mac, french fries and a Coke. She sat by the window, chewing on the food, and watching the shadows lengthen on the street outside, until dusk began to fall.

By the time she'd finished, the one thing clear in her mind was that if she truly loved Morgan, wanted a future with him, she'd simply have to bury her pride, put aside all the knotty reservations about his refusal to discuss the past, and make the best of it. She had no idea what exactly it was she intended to do, only that it had to be something. And soon.

Glancing out of the window, she was surprised to see that it had grown quite dark. Since this wasn't the best neighborhood for a woman to be out alone in at night, she hurriedly gathered up her rubbish, threw it into the garbage bin, and went back out on to the pavement, heading toward home.

As she approached her building, half a block away, in the dim light cast by the streetlight a few doors down, she could see two men lingering at the foot of the stairs leading up to her front doorstep. Immediately, she began to slow her steps, a sudden sharp stab of sheer terror clutching at the pit of her stomach. Muggings, even actual rapes, were unpleasant facts of life in the big city, so that no woman alone could afford to ignore the dangers.

She moved closer to the kerb. There was still quite a bit of traffic going by. The area wasn't quite deserted. Surely, she had nothing to fear. She quickened her step, clutching her handbag more tightly, and keeping a close eye on the two men.

It wasn't until she was directly in front of the building, her key already out of her bag and in her hand, that she recognized Morgan. Her heart gave a great leap. But who was the man with him?

Morgan had seen her now, and had come down to the bottom of the steps to stand on the pavement, waiting for her. He began to walk slowly toward her, and as their eyes met and held together, she hurried a little faster until at last they were face-to-face.

"Nora . . ." he began, gazing down at her.

"Morgan . . ." she said, at the same time.

They smiled at each other. Then, as though it were the most natural thing in the world, she found herself in his arms. The intervening months apart since their last time together simply slipped away, and she nestled happily against his broad chest. This was where she belonged, where she was meant to be.

After a few moments, she heard a discreet cough coming from behind him. She drew her head back, and looked past his shoulder to see the other man walking toward them. Then, as he came closer, she recognized him. It was Morgan's father! What was he doing here? Obviously Morgan had brought him, but why?

Morgan glanced back at the older man, then turned back to Nora. "Nora," he said gravely. "I'd like to introduce my father, Neil Latimer. This is Nora Graham."

"Pleased to meet you, Nora," Neil Latimer said. "Morgan tells me you're doing great work for his company."

They chatted for a few moments about the commercial she was getting together for Latimer's. He made no reference to their earlier meeting on Christmas Eve, and Nora was just as glad not to have to discuss the painful subject.

"Well," he announced abruptly, "I think I'll be running along. You two don't need me for company, and I told Anne I'd be back by ten o'clock to relieve the sitter."

He raised a hand to hail a passing taxi, leaving Morgan and Nora standing alone at the kerb looking after him. When the taxi had disappeared from view, he turned to her.

Nora searched his face, waiting for him to speak. She was certain that he had a definite purpose in bringing his father here to meet her tonight, that it was a symbolic gesture of some kind, even a concession to her that must have cost him a great deal. But she couldn't get her hopes raised too high.

"Can we go inside?" he said, after a moment. "I'd like to talk to you."

She nodded, and they went up the steps. She unlocked the front door, and he followed her down the hall. Neither of them spoke a word as they went, but the electricity between them was building to such a pitch of intensity that by the time they were inside her flat Nora's knees were almost buckling under her.

She closed the door and turned to him. "I'm glad to see that you've made things up with your father," she said carefully.

"Well, I wouldn't go that far," he replied with a wry smile. "But we've had some good talks."

"That's wonderful," she said. "And has it helped?"

"Well, I've finally been able at least to listen to his version of what happened so long ago. It never even occurred to me that the reason he'd kept so silent about my mother, what she did, was that he didn't want to spoil my fantasies about her." He winced with pain. "Actually, I think underneath I always knew the truth about her, that she'd abandoned us. Any other version would have shattered the fairy tale, the excuse she must have had for leaving. I think that's what I couldn't bear, that she'd not only left him, but me as well."

"Oh, Morgan, I'm so sorry," she murmured, her heart aching for him.

He waved a hand in the air. "It's ancient history. I just should have had the sense to deal with it long ago." He smiled bleakly. "At least I understand him much better now. Although I still don't think he was any great shakes as a father, I do realize that he was a disappointed man. Everything he turned his hand to failed. Then when she left him to raise three kids on his own, he couldn't cope." He smiled ruefully. "I guess he did his best, though, stuck it out until we were grown, saw that we were fed, and clothed, and educated."

"And you have to give him credit for that," she said softly.

He nodded. "Yes. I have to do that. In any event, facing the truth has made me realize why I couldn't trust myself ever to love a woman again." He shrugged. "That's what women did, in my mind. Left the men who loved them."

"So you made up your mind you had to leave them first."

He nodded grimly. "Something like that."

Seeing him like this, so wounded, so raw and vulnerable, aroused an overwhelming tenderness in Nora. For such a strong man to admit his own weakness surely took enormous courage.

"It can't be easy to see one's most cherished illusions crumble," she said gravely. "I think you're doing a very brave thing just by facing up to the fact that it *was* all an illusion."

"It's a start, anyway. Thanks largely to you." His face crumpled, and he reached out for her.

"Oh, Morgan," she breathed, and fell into his arms.

"Good grief, I've been such a fool," he breathed in her ear. "I was so afraid I'd lost you for good, that I'd never hold you like this again." He buried his head in her hair. "To think that I let you get away just because you cared enough about me to make me face myself!"

She raised her head. "Do you really believe that now?"

He nodded gravely. "If it hadn't been for you I never would have come to terms with the past. I've been like a blind man all these years, feeding on a fantasy that had nothing to do with what really happened, nursing resentment against the one man who at least tried to meet his responsibilities." He shook his head. "I'd become so used to locking up my feelings in order to keep that fantasy alive that I didn't dare reveal them, even to myself."

"Then you're not angry at me for prying?"

"Of course not! You were right all along." He wrinkled his forehead in a worried frown. "It's not too late for us, is it, Nora? Tell me I haven't spoiled things for good." He hesitated. "You said once that you loved me. Do you still care for me at all?"

Their eyes met and locked together. "Oh, yes," she whispered. "I do. I never stopped loving you."

"Oh, darling," he groaned, pulling her more tightly up against him. "I love you so much."

Nora clung to him with all her strength as he stroked her hair, her shoulders, her back. Then his lips found hers, and he kissed her as though he wanted to devour her.

Finally, he tore his mouth from hers and gazed down at her. "I was so afraid I'd lost you," he said brokenly.

"Never, darling," she whispered, putting a hand on his face. "Never."

"And you promise you'll marry me?"

She smiled up at him, her face glowing, then reached for one of his hands, and placed it on her breast. "Of course I'll marry you, darling. Any time, any place."

The hand on her breast began to move. Slowly, rhythmically, he kneaded the soft mounds until she moaned deep in her throat at the sensations those magic fingers aroused in her. Then his hands came up to cradle her face, the fingers tracing every line and feature.

"I want you," he murmured.

She smiled up at him. "I know, darling. I want you, too."

Slowly, the glittering gray eyes never leaving hers, he reached out and began to unbutton her blouse.

With ever downward motion his hand pressed against her, heightening her desire, until the last button was undone and he slid the blouse off her shoulders and down over her arms.

She stood motionless before him and watched the silvery eyes grow brighter as they drank in her bare shoulders, and the wispy flesh-colored bra, the smooth skin above the waistband of her skirt. He raised both his hands and ran the tips of his fingers very lightly over the hard points of her breasts, back and forth, then in a slow circular motion, until the ache became unbearable.

"Oh, Morgan, please," she choked out, her eyes pleading.

He smiled, and undid the clasp of her bra. As he pulled the straps down, his hands brushed against the burning naked flesh, and she closed her eyes in an agony of longing.

"You're so beautiful, darling," she heard him murmur.

She threw her head back, her full breasts filling his waiting hands, then felt his head came down to place his moist lips over one taut nipple, his softly rasping tongue bathing it gently.

Finally, she couldn't bear it another moment. She put her hands on the dark head at her breast, pressing it to her, then raised it up, and looked into his eyes. She reached out and started to undo his shirt, then the buckle of his belt. Then, pressing herself up against him, she threw her arms around his neck, and slowly, they moved down the hall, as though in a dance.

In her bedroom, she lay on the bed watching him in the glow of the dim light burning in the hall, as he hurriedly tore his clothes off, until finally the hard-muscled body was revealed before her in all its splendor.

In the split second before he slid onto the bed beside her and took her in his arms, she thought fleetingly of the conversation she'd had with Anne that day. Miracles did happen after all.

New York Times Bestselling Author

Sandra Brown

Tomorrow's Promise

**She cherished the memory
of love but was consumed
by a new passion too
fierce to ignore.**

For Keely Preston, the memory of her husband
Mark has been frozen in time since the day he was
listed as missing in action. And now, twelve years
later, twenty-six men listed as MIA have been
found.

Keely's torn between hope for Mark and despair
for herself. Because now, after all the years of
waiting, she has met another man!

**Don't miss TOMORROW'S PROMISE by
SANDRA BROWN.**

**Available in June wherever Harlequin
books are sold.**

HARLEQUIN ROMANCE®

Let Harlequin Romance® take you

BACK TO THE

Come to the Kincaid Ranch, near Red Horse, Wyoming.

Meet rancher Ethan Kincaid and a woman named Maggie Deaton—ex-rancher and ex-convict!

Read THE BAD PENNY by Susan Fox—her first Harlequin Romance in 4 years! Available in June 1993 wherever Harlequin books are sold.

RANCH1